THE
BARATARIA KEY

J.M. RICHARDSON

Winter Goose
PUBLISHING
where words take flight

Winter Goose Publishing
45 Lafayette Road #114
North Hampton, NH 03862

www.wintergoosepublishing.com
Contact Information: info@wintergoosepublishing.com

The Barataria Key

COPYRIGHT © 2016 by J. M. Richardson

First Edition, December 2016

Cover Design by Winter Goose Publishing
Typesetting by Odyssey Books

ISBN: 978-1-941058-53-4

Published in the United States of America

ALSO BY J.M. RICHARDSON

The Twenty-Nine
The Apocalypse Mechanism
A Line in the Sand

For Audrey and Elle
Their youth inspires the spirit of adventure

Prologue

September 3, 1814

The schooner pitched and rolled from side to side as it crashed against the swells. Salty gulf water splashed upward over the *Petite Milan*'s sturdy wooden bow and onto the deck and the men who scurried across it. A rhythmic symphony of motion and spray accompanied the diligent work of all sailors, who seemed to orbit around the captain and his first mate like they were some gravitational cosmic force.

The captain was as a statue, virtually unmoved in his pose near the port side rail. His beaten and weathered black hat remained stationary with a single white plume that swished with the wind. His lean frame was draped in a loose and untied white shirt that exposed his chest hair amid flapping cotton material. Dingy black trousers became knee-high leather boots worn by salty air and maritime abuse.

His scruffy, unshaven face was devoid of emotion. He peered through his spyglass into the distant haze as his first mate looked on with despair. But the captain did not move, nor did his expression change even with the silhouette of the much larger and more superior gunboat in the distance, its British Union Jack dancing in the wind.

"The British, Captain?" the first mate implored in their native French.

"Oui," he answered, as he lowered his spyglass but kept a watchful eye on the distant ship.

"What shall we—"

The first mate's question was interrupted as they both saw a small flash from the British gunboat. A few moments passed before they heard the thunderous, yet distant roar of the cannon. It was then that the rest of the crew ceased their activities and beamed out across the water. A sudden splash erupted ahead of the bow like a strange oceanic geyser.

"Mon dieu!" The first mate cringed.

"It's just a warning shot, you coward," the captain scoffed. "They want us to yield."

The captain turned his head once more to face the deadly ship on the horizon. He was silent for many moments, a scowl on his face. His eyebrows lowered into a *V* shape that indented the skin between. The lines around his mouth and nose somehow deepened into ravines beneath his stubble. He crossed his arms as his spyglass hung from his hand.

"We can outrun them, but not indefinitely," he told his first mate without looking at him. "Head for Barataria. Ground the ship in the shallows. Those English dogs and their heavy ship will not be able to even come close to the island. If their captain requests an audience with me, they can come to us, and in small numbers. They'll do it on *our* terms."

"Yes, Captain," the first mate responded, and left his side to deliver the orders that sent the men aboard *Petit Milan* to prepare all sails. They caught the gulf winds, and felt a sudden boost of speed as the schooner blazed into Barataria Bay and into the marshes.

"They're fleeing into the swamps," British Army Captain McWilliams called out over the winds as he stood to the side of the ship's captain. "Cowards, the lot of them."

"No," the ship's commander, Captain Nicholas Lockyer, said as he lowered his spyglass. He smiled, though no one could tell. His aging face hung with a bit of extra skin, which concealed many emotions and their manifestations. His dark blue coat was pristine and decorated heavily upon the left breast. A large cocked hat crested his fluffy, powdered white wig as he exuded power and high birth over everyone on the ship. He collapsed his polished brass spyglass, and continued. "Brilliant. These brigands want us to chase them into the shallows, and then anchor. They want to force us to meet them without troops."

"That's madness," McWilliams burst. "Surely they don't expect us to fall for that."

"Prepare to enter the bay!" Lockyer yelled his command as men readied the sails and took the helm. "Get a boat ready to row ashore!"

"Captain, you can't possibly—" McWilliams was cut short.

"We have orders, my good man. I intend to follow them. It is our duty," he reaffirmed, and left his army counterpart with a gaping, silent mouth.

Dolphins leapt from the water at the bow as the *HMS Sophie*'s deep keel cut through the rough swells with ease. She entered Barataria Bay, past Isle Grand Terre to her port side. *What a forsaken place this is*, Lockyer thought as he viewed the place from the railing. There was no beauty to it as he had seen in the Eastern Caribbean. There were no exotic jungles and wildlife; no towering, mist-blanketed mountains. This barrier island's shrub-topped inland dunes were surrounded by rather dreary beaches and water filled with the mud and silt that constantly spilled out of the Mississippi and Atchafalaya deltas.

Barataria Bay was no better. The brown, brackish water jumped with mullets' scaly ballet and the air teemed with seagulls and brown pelicans. Small, flat marsh islands, waterlogged and covered with coastal grasses, dotted the area in a scene that no one aboard the *Sophie* had ever witnessed. To them, it was a wasteland reserved for primitive people.

But where fresh bayous poured into the marsh, lofty cypress and oak trees stood half covered in dangling, curly Spanish moss. Cicadas in the muddy wetland forest welcomed the coming evening. It appeared ancient and undisturbed, like a forgotten Eden in the coastal United States.

"Sir," came a nervous voice as the ship's first mate appeared at the captain's side. "We're beginning to drag the mud beneath us. It's low tide. Shall we drop anchor?"

"Yes," Lockyer confirmed as he kept an eye on the island ahead. "That's the schooner there; aground at that island. Drop anchor and prepare the dinghy and a white flag."

"Should we blast them out of the water, sir?" a man at the water's edge asked his captain in French. He and several other men who occupied the island stood and watched as a dinghy filled with redcoats rowed ever closer beneath a small pole and white flag. "Who knows what treasures could be aboard—and weapons."

"When did we become barbarians?" he answered in his native tongue. "They fly a white flag. They are our guests, and we will greet them as such. Fetch me five good men. The six of you will accompany me on a skiff to meet them."

The light of the sun dimmed as it sunk further below the oaks and cypresses. The rays cut between the trees like horizontal beams that illuminated the rising vapor. The two small craft neared as each band of men carefully examined the other. All rowing stopped and the boats coasted together as one man on each stood and leaned over the bow to unite them. The sailors from the island narrowed their eyes and sneered at the other men. The British seemed appalled at the sight and stench of the French sailors who had rowed out to them.

"We have specific orders." Captain Lockyer stood slowly. "Orders to bring a packet of letters to The Commodore of Barataria," he said nervously.

The French-speaking sailors erupted into laughter as a pack of mangy hyenas and joked to themselves in their own language. After several moments, they allowed their amusement to calm and returned their gaze to the foreign sailors and soldiers.

"Should we have brought an interpreter?" Captain Lockyer looked around to his men.

"No need." The French captain spoke in English, yet with quite a heavy dialect of his own tongue. "We will take you to the," he snickered, "Commodore of Barataria. Follow us," he said as they unhitched the boats and rowed back toward the island.

"I do not have a pleasant feeling about this, Lockyer," McWilliams uttered as he shook his head in worry.

As each small boat ran aground onto the shore of the Island of Barataria, the sun had set with a dark blanket over the land, and the men on dry ground had already lit a number of torches and campfires in the villa of shacks in the background. Fear shivered the hearts of each of the British men as they knew they had officially reached enemy territory without the weapons of the might of His Majesty's Navy. Countless tattered ruffians puffed away on pipes and eased their hands closer to their weapons in anticipation as the British were led further into the silent crowd. Their bright red coats became beacons to violence even in the evening darkness.

Then the crowd grew less silent. It started with the small sounds of a few daggers unsheathed and flint-lock pistols cocked and readied. The sound grew as similar noises multiplied. As Captain McWilliams turned, his skin chilled in the September humidity to see an ocean of sneering thugs who brandished their blades and aimed their pistols at the small band of British soldiers.

"What are you doing?" the French captain turned to question his own followers in their language. "There will be no bloodshed here today."

"I already have a cypress tree picked out," a large man growled at his captain as he stepped from the shadows with a noose in his hand. "I say we hang these English dogs and feed them to the alligators!"

The redcoats quivered as they watched this man. They weren't sure exactly what he said, but the tone of his voice, the noose in his hand, along with the cheers of agreement that rippled throughout the crowd, told them all they needed to know.

"No," the French captain asserted, and stepped toward the angry man and his lynch mob. "I will not have it. And any man who dares challenge me will meet the same fate that you propose for our guests. Henri, Antoine, and Jacques—guard the door to my home," he ordered as he led the men closer to the door of the largest building in the villa.

"Are you the . . ." a surprised Captain McWilliams began to ask as they neared the door.

"Commodore?" The captain grinned, amused with that word. "I suppose. I am Captain Jean Lafitte, at your service," he said, and removed his hat and bowed with exaggeration as if he were on stage, before he opened the door and led the men inside.

He guided in the two British officers and four unarmed soldiers, escorted by two of his own men. The fire crackled in the hearth to the left and very dimly illuminated the trappings of such a humble swamp shack. A long cypress table and two benches lay at the focal point of the single room. A few silver candelabras held unlit candles that stemmed high above the table. Upon the wall hung a sizable portrait of some unnamed noblewoman in a wig. The corner of the rustic space held a lavish, ornate bed.

Lafitte did not even slow his gait as he strolled past the table and grasped one of the candelabras, lighting the candles in the fire. He then carried it across the wooden floor boards and placed it upon the table. He took a seat with a motion that his guests should do the same.

"Would you care for a smoke, gentlemen?" he offered, and then struck a match to light his pipe, which filled the air with a strange, non-tobacco odor. "Turkish hashish. The best I've ever had," he said in French-glazed English.

Neither British commander spoke. They just stared at the man before them and shook their heads in decline. They marveled at this man. He appeared no better than the ruffians outside who salivated for English blood. Yet, he had smoothness in his demeanor and temperament uncommon in this type of rogue. He was almost pleasant, gentlemanly, and cordial in his treatment of them thus far. But they could tell he had charisma. His men loved him.

"Well, your loss." Lafitte took in the deep burn of smoke and exhaled with enjoyment.

"You are the pirate Jean Lafitte?" Lockyer inquired quite bluntly.

"Pirate?" Lafitte scoffed with a smile. "To the contrary, gentlemen, I am but a privateer. I have letters of marque from Cartagena to plunder the ships of her enemies. You saw my flags, yet I speak French. I am a privateer—a businessman."

"But you do not possess letters of marque from the British crown, and so, in the eyes of Parliament and His Majesty, you are, indeed, a pirate," Lockyer argued.

"I do not answer to the laws of your king." Lafitte lost his patience and his smile.

"Wait, Captain Lafitte," McWilliams stopped as he sensed the tension grow. "Perhaps we began wrong. What if you were offered something better than letters of marque?"

Lafitte calmed a bit, and continued to smoke his pipe as he lowered his eyes to the packet on the table before the captain. McWilliams slid the bundle of two envelopes across the splintering wood of the tabletop. Lafitte untied the crimson ribbon that bound them. He extracted the first letter, which was closed under the seal of King George III. He unfolded it and then took a few moments to read it.

"Interesting." Lafitte's eyebrows rose. "You appear to be planning an attack on the city of New Orleans by year's end."

"We will control the most important shipping route in the whole of the United States," Lockyer interjected.

"And your king wants my help on the naval end of it." Lafitte stared at the letter and puffed his pipe. "In exchange for estates in England for my brother Pierre and I," he read on. "I'm assuming that you will free him from prison once you have taken the city."

"Indeed, sir," McWilliams agreed.

"Would I not be a traitor to my French roots?"

"It does not appear that you have any clear allegiances to anyone but yourself and your men as it is," McWilliams said. "You would just be looking out for yourself. You said you were a businessman."

"And my men?"

"They would receive letters of marque from the king, and be authorized to plunder any non-British ship in the Gulf of Mexico, sell the booty, and pay a tribute to the crown."

"Sounds enticing." Lafitte set down the letter and contemplated. "And what is this other letter?"

"One from my superior commander urging you to take the deal," McWilliams replied.

"There is another matter," Lockyer spoke freely. "I was asked to question you about the plundering of a British gunship near Pensacola some three years ago. Her name was the *HMS Danbury*."

"Danbury, Danbury." Lafitte feigned contemplation, as if he could not remember.

"She carried a very precious cargo confiscated from a Spanish ship off the coast of British Honduras," Lockyer reminded him as McWilliams looked on without a clue as to what this was about.

"Ah, I remember this one." Lafitte smiled to one of his men. "Lots of Spanish gold doubloons. Strange cargo aboard this ship," he laughed.

"Keep the gold." Lockyer became stern. "There was something else aboard."

"Oh, you mean that worthless piece of stone found in a locked box in the captain's quarters." He continued to smile and set down his empty pipe.

"Do you still have it?" Lockyer raised his voice with urgency.

"I nearly threw it overboard upon first looking at it." Lafitte grinned as Lockyer's face turned bright red. "Worthless jaguar figurine. What use could that be to me? But considering that my men had to cut through five armed guards to get to it, I was interested. And then there was the page from the Spanish captain's log tucked into the box. And that *really* intrigued me."

"My king would pay handsomely for its return."

"Sold it." Lafitte put it bluntly. "Sold at one of my auctions at the Temple. It didn't fetch much money, either. I think we sold it to some Creole man. He said it was to be a birthday gift for his eight-year-old son."

Lockyer turned red with fury, something that Lafitte and his men quite enjoyed. The dynamic of the situation was pure entertainment. Here was a man with a short temper, ready to unleash a stream of obscenities at the privateer men, yet he was forced to keep his anger subdued for fear of retaliation by scores of blood-thirsty pirate followers just beyond the door.

"Consider our offer," McWilliams pleaded, unnerved by the secrecy of this unnamed object of which Lockyer had spoken.

"And if I do not?" Laffite countered.

"Then the British Navy will descend upon this island and destroy you all." Lockyer finally unleashed the building steam from beneath his wig and bright gold medals.

"Our meeting is over." Lafitte stood abruptly, as he smiled and motioned toward the door. "They are not to be harmed!" He reverted to French in his orders to his most trusted men. "Escort them to their boat, provide them a torch, and see to it they push off safely."

"Consider it, Captain," McWilliams said one last time as he was ushered out the door.

As the door closed and latched, Lafitte was left alone with his first mate. His face, nearly orange in the light of the hearth fire and candles, turned from amusement to concern and contemplation. He walked across the room to his bed and stopped just short of it to kneel down and remove a loose board from the floor beneath the bed. He carefully extracted a small wooden box and opened it to reveal an intricately carved piece of stone in the likeness of a fearsome Central American jaguar.

Lafitte stared at it for some time, allowing himself to take in every detail. It called to him. It did every night in his dreams. He would run through the jungles, stalked by the giant jungle cat. Or he would follow it down a path where it might stand and just leer at him. But now, it seemed to call out a warning. It begged him not to be sold to the British.

"Captain?" His first mate's voice shook him from the trance. "What shall we do?"

"Contact Governor Claiborne," he said as he slammed the box shut. "We will warn the Americans."

Chapter 1

Bare feet creaked and popped the crimson-stained floor planks, a hollow resonance beneath them like notes within an acoustic guitar. Attached to those feet, two legs clad in a loose purple pair of LSU pajama pants trudged along. James Beauregard lifted a hand above his bare toned torso, and scratched his tussled hair.

James was made more alert by the wonderful aromas dancing through the air. Noelle, he could see through his blurry sleep eyes, moved about the kitchen with perk. Her dark brown hair draped over her shoulders as satin curtains and her usual pink silk pajamas covered, but accentuated, her modest curves.

"Good morning, baby," she said as she caught a glimpse of James from the corner of her eye.

"Good morning," he responded. "Is that the good Congo stuff?" He motioned toward the coffee still percolating in the modern steel pot across the kitchen.

"Yup." She wiped flour from the polished granite countertops. "Would you like me to make you a cup?"

"Sure." He leaned on the bar that overlooked the kitchen and nudged aside a stack of bridal magazines, all of which had become worn and wrinkled. "I was thinking of ordering some kopi luwak offline."

"Online," she shot back.

"What?"

"From online. Not offline."

"Whatever," he said, and rolled his eyes.

"Kopi lu-what?" she puzzled, yet never looked up.

"Kopi luwak. It's an Indonesian coffee—the most expensive in the world. It's six hundred dollars a pound."

"Jesus!" Her brow lowered. "What makes it so special? Must be good."

"It's shit."

"Well, then why buy it?"

"No, literally, it's shit," he clarified. "The beans are eaten by some kind of cat-like creature, and then the cat shits it out in little turds that look like Payday bars. It's cleaned and the beans in the turd are roasted and ground."

"Buy whatever you want." She shook her head. "You're the publishing heir. It's your money. Just don't expect me to drink it." She then smiled. "You hate being out of the classroom. Always trying to teach me something."

Noelle removed the heavy stainless steel coffee pot from its cradle, and poured James a voluminous amount of dark roasted Congolese coffee into the biggest mug in the house, the *Neanderthal mug*. It steamed upward with a swirl until a little cream and two teaspoons of sugar were added. She set it in front of him with a ceramic clink. A quick kiss, and then she turned with a smile. She grabbed two red pot holders from the countertop. As she opened the oven below her, James admired her gifted posterior.

"Biscuit?" She removed the pan, and placed it upon the vacant cook top with a light clang. "My grand-mère's recipe, God rest her soul." She crossed herself and peered upward.

"Sure," he said, delighted at the sight of the biscuits. "My, you *have* been up awhile."

"Yeah. Always happens during the break." She shrugged. "I get into the routine of getting up early, and while I'm off I can't seem to sleep late."

"Oh no," James disagreed. "When Christmas or spring break rolls around, I sleep late. All these snotty grad students are getting on my nerves lately."

"Take some time off," she said, placing a couple of biscuits on a paper plate for her fiancé, and slipping them across the bar to him. "You're the top shareholder in a publishing company your grandfather started. You don't need Tulane's paycheck."

"I don't know. I'd miss it," he said with a mouth half filled with biscuit. "You said so yourself."

"I'm quite happy where I am," she interjected. "Snotty Tulane geology students beat snotty Yale geology students any day of the week."

James set his half-empty mug of coffee on the bar and circled around to meet her in the kitchen. He placed his hands on the silky curves of her hips as she threw her arms around his neck. They enjoyed each other's lips and warmth for several moments in silence, always thankful for one another.

"First day of spring break, future Mrs. Beauregard," he said, breaking the silence. "What shall we do today? Sit around all day in our underwear? Maybe less?"

"I'm keeping my maiden name, remember?" She lowered her tone and her brow.

"I know, I know," he laughed. "But seriously. Let's just sit around all day with nothing on. And just watch . . . game shows or something."

"Tempting." She bit her lip. "But sorry, I have to work today."

"Work?" he frowned. "It's spring break. Let's go down to Florida and party it up or something."

"I got a call from the dean of the geology department this morning. That's a huge deal."

"A call for what?"

"Something happened last night in Jackson Square," she shrugged. "Subsidence issues. Apparently, the statue of Jackson sunk into the ground all of a sudden, and the city wants a team from our geology department there to supervise the investigation."

"Wow, that's crazy." He took another hot sip of coffee.

"Yeah, turn on the TV—I'm sure it's all over the local morning news." Noelle motioned toward the small television on the far end of the kitchen counter.

James eyed the screen for a moment and willed it to turn on, almost as if he wished it to do so by itself or through telepathy. Something told him that would not happen, so he searched for the remote control. He scanned the polished granite countertop and its trappings in vain, for the little chunk of plastic was nowhere to be seen. Pressurized frustration edged the gauge needles into the red. Noelle seemed nervous.

His management of his own emotions needed work, but he was getting better. He turned to alcohol much less frequently than he used to—tried to find more constructive outlets. He was happier. He seemed to have moved on from the anguish of losing his family.

Still, the frustration and anxiety mounted with sometimes even the smallest setback. It was overload, and the pressure had to go somewhere. He turned frantic in his search for the remote control, sliding aside bins of utensils and junk mail that had not been thrown out.

"You could just walk over and turn it on manually," she nearly whispered, a little grin on her face.

James did not answer; only resorted to checking drawers he knew could never be the remote control's hiding place. He pulled the drawer with the pot holders and dish rags. The one filled with silverware. He rolled his eyes at his own absent-mindedness and realized that if he were going to check the drawers, he should have started with the junk drawer. He opened it with reluctance, as he knew he would be frustrated.

Jesus Christ, he felt it coming on.

"What the hell?" His eyes widened as he pulled it open. "What is the remote doing in the junk drawer?" He removed it from atop a graveyard of batteries of undeterminable charge levels and pens that no longer worked.

"I was cleaning up, and the remote needed a home so it wouldn't get anything spilled on it," she defended.

"Oh," he said as he calmed down. "Good call. Sorry." He retracted his rant and pressed the red power button to click on the kitchen TV.

It was already set on the local Channel 4 station, and as the picture brightened, the view they expected appeared. The aerial helicopter shot was zoomed in on Jackson Square so that the Cabildo, Presbytere, and St. Louis Cathedral were obscured. Spring had taken hold of the park. Leaves had returned to the trees and flowers blossomed and bloomed in the bushes planted near the statue. But it was not a normal scene in any way. It was more of a murder scene, and in New Orleans, it might as well have been. Yellow police tape tied to wooden stakes formed a perimeter meant to keep away tourists and onlookers who clicked away with their camera phones. Police officers stood guard to make sure no one got in for a closer look. In the heart of the police tape perimeter, city officials and engineers stood around in puzzlement over the spectacle.

The centerpiece of Jackson Square, the equestrian statue of Andrew Jackson tipping his hat to the west, was sunken into the ground by over ten feet by James's estimation. Its huge granite base was almost invisible beneath the soggy Crescent City soil. It was tilted deeper in the back where the only two grounded hooves nearly touched the grass. It was odd—something that had always been there and appeared a certain way was so drastically changed that it even caused him anxiety. Change frightened him.

"Holy shit!" He gaped at the sight as he ignored the commentary by the news anchors. "That's what you're doing this morning?"

"Yup. Cool, huh?"

"Can I tag along?" He slid her way, his hands around her waist.

"Did you forget that you have plans this morning, too?" she cooed as she wreathed her own arms around his muscular neck and shoulders.

"What?" His brow curled down in the middle as he tried to remember.

"You have a date with Louis Armstrong."

"Louis Arm . . . Oh. Oh crap, I forgot. The airport."

"Yeah," she burst with amusement. "How could you forget that we have a guest this week? Tim Horn's flight comes in at ten thirty a.m."

"Oh, I forgot about that." He released her and shook his head. "I don't know why. I just did."

She took a final sip of her coffee and turned to approach the pot for a refill. She let the dark, hot liquid flow into her cup and then took a big bite out of one of her special biscuits.

"I'm so glad you two made up."

"Well, it's taken a long time," he nodded. "But I've learned over the last few years to put the past behind me. It's hard to forget what he did."

"But you forgave."

"Not for his sake," he nodded. "For mine. So *I* can move on. So *I* can live *my* life. And," he shrugged, "I guess it's been nice to have an old friend back."

"Well said," she said, and patted his arm as she passed him. "Now, if I were you, I'd go get a shower and get going."

"Yeah," he said absently as he stared in disbelief at the scene of Jackson Square.

Chapter 2

Here they come, James thought to himself as he leaned against his silver Tahoe in the pick-up lane of New Orleans International Airport. *Stupid spring-breakers.*

He scowled in contempt as he watched college-aged boys file out of the automatic metal doors to the airport. Many of them packed light—everything they needed in a large backpack. They would re-wear some of their party clothes from earlier in the week—anything that saves them the money in checking their bags. Those clothes would all have the distinct smell of smoke and alcohol at the end of the night anyway, so it didn't matter whether or not they were clean.

The female groups weren't much different. They packed significantly heavier than the boys, with much more need for diversity in their garment selections. They had to bring perfumes and flat irons for their hair. They needed lotions and several choices of shoes. By contrast, they travelled with the comfort and the look of having just emerged from their dorm room beds—tanks, sweats, and no makeup under oversized sunglasses. They were on a collision course with each other, an experience that was an alcohol- and sex-filled rite of passage for the American college kid.

Why can't they just go to the beach like everyone else? But the city needed tourism revenue. What he really hated about spring-breakers was the general disrespect shown to the city. To them, New Orleans may as well be Las Vegas, and it was if you added nearly three hundred years of cultural gumbo and unique architecture not found anywhere else in the country. Each night these kids would hit Bourbon Street and recklessly swill amounts of alcohol they were not used to. They would urinate on someone's doorstep and vomit in the street gutters before passing out in their hotel rooms and sleeping until mid-afternoon. When they awoke, no one would see a museum or stroll down Royal

Street to admire the architecture. No photos in Jackson Square or visits to St. Louis Cathedral. They would end their spring break never having heard words like *Cabildo* or *French Market*. No fine Creole cuisine. Just the same fast food eateries found in their own college towns.

Screw it. Let 'em be kids. He thought back to his college days. He tried to change his thought process, as it polluted his mood. *Maybe Tim's flight got cancelled and I can just go home and sleep.*

But then he caught a glimpse of Tim Horn as he exited the airport doors. He moved with confidence, his semi-curly black hair waving with the breeze. He grinned as he placed his dark sunglasses upon the bridge of his nose, and turned his gaze to the plump, tight rear ends of the coeds to his right. He strutted with the swagger of a rock star in the body of a Yale professor.

He coolly looked around for a moment to scan the taxis and minivans that rolled and parked under the concrete covering to the arrival pick-up lanes. He watched as spring-breakers packed taxi trunks with their luggage and families embraced with relatives they had not seen in some time. And then his eyes met with James's as a cocky smile followed. He strolled up, his brown wing-tip dress shoes causing echo as an audible testimony to his style.

"Jimbo, Jimbo, Jimbo!" Tim gushed as he grasped James's hand and pulled him in for an awkward slap on the back. "How the hell are ya?"

"Not bad." James opened the back hatch of the SUV as Tim headed to the back of the vehicle and hoisted up his suitcase. "We've got to get the hell out of here. The TSA Nazi over there has been shooting me the stink eye for the past fifteen minutes."

The two men hopped into the upscale Tahoe and found comfort in the black leather. James glanced to his right to see his estranged friend still staring across the curb at the young coeds who piled into the taxi. He almost salivated the way a dog does in a kitchen while his master flips the breakfast bacon in the skillet.

"God, I missed New Orleans!" Tim never turned his attention away from the girls as the Tahoe moved along the airport lanes. "And it looks like I picked the right time of year to make a comeback."

"You know you probably out-age those kids by about fifteen years," James scolded. "You're a professor, for God's sake."

"Hey, they're not *my* students, and they're of age," Tim chuckled. "There is nothing unethical about it."

"Well either way, to her, you're an old fart, whether you're forty yet or not," James fired back. "They're out of your league, brother."

"You'd be surprised how many college girls appreciate the sophistication and worldliness of an older Yale professor—think it's sexy, even. It's nature. Biologically, they're looking for a provider with good genes, and I'm looking for a young, fertile woman with—"

"I get it," James laughed.

"So what are we getting into this week?" He clapped and rubbed his hands together. "Bourbon Street? Uptown? Hit it old-school?"

"I was thinking dinner and a glass of wine," James replied.

"Oh, Jesus Christ! When did you grow up on me? It's spring break, buddy."

"And I have a fiancée."

"So she won't let you off the leash, huh?" Tim jeered.

"It's not that," he defended. "She'll likely be all about going out with us, but we've kind of changed the venues we usually frequent."

"Well, it looks like I'm going to have to work on her later."

James frowned while his thoughts drifted and his mood soured. He could not help the onslaught of thoughts and emotions associated with the last time Timothy Horn had visited him in New Orleans. That was years ago, and the friendship ended when he made a sexual advance on his now dead wife.

The interior of the SUV fell awkwardly silent, though "awkward" was not in Tim's vocabulary. He said what he wanted, when he wanted, without fear of repercussion. In a way, James admired that. He wished sometimes he could be like that. There was a sense of freedom in it—freedom of cultural norms and social cues. That was just the way Tim was, and people either loved him or hated him. But now he picked up on the awkwardness, and in the interest of saving this friendship, he said nothing more.

James fought the emotion. He wanted to save the friendship as much as Tim did. It was easy to click and confirm a friend request or comment lightheartedly on one another's status updates. An otherwise two-minute conversation took hours, or even days, to complete, which allowed both parties to carefully formulate what to say to one another before a post. But face-to-face was more difficult. There was an added level of complexity and social choreography with emotions, facial expressions, and body language to observe. There was meaning in the tone of the voice.

A sudden noise jolted the mood with electronic sharpness. James's phone played its usual ringtone: Seventies-style porn music reminiscent of thick mustaches and glimmering mirror balls. Tim giggled at the music as James took his eyes off the interstate to view the phone on the rubber inset of the center console. His eyes shot back and forth from the road to the phone in an attempt to make out the name on the front display screen. His eyes lit up as they always did when she called, and he picked up the phone.

"Hey, baby." He watched Tim roll his eyes. "How is it going in Jackson Square?"

"Actually, I'm back at the university," she said. "In *your* department with *your* dean."

"Why?"

"They got the crane hooked up to the statue and lifted it out of the hole, and of course my people started getting in there to examine the subsidence problem. Engineers were trying to figure out how to fix it, etc. And then I spotted something as I was digging around."

"I knew it," he smiled. "Mutant moles double the normal size dug out a hole under the statue! Did you find the nest?"

"You goober," she laughed. "No, jackass, a box. An iron box. It's probably been down there since . . ."

"Eighteen fifty-three. That's how long the statue has been there."

"Okay, sure. Either way, we brought it to the history department and they got someone to open it up. There's something really cool inside, so get your ass down here pronto."

"What is it?" he asked with excitement.

"You'll have to see when you get here. Bye." A click indicated she had hung up.

"Shit." He looked at the blinking call duration and set down the phone. "Up for making a stop at Tulane?" He shot a glance over at his friend, finally feeling a little better.

"Why not?"

The Tahoe moved along Interstate 10, which cut down through the Metairie suburbs, ever closer to downtown. This, while in college in Baton Rouge, was always the home stretch. Beyond, the light haze veiled the downtown skyline, complete with the Superdome centerpiece in the foreground. All around, on either side of the highway, little white and gray buildings formed an expansive city of the dead. These mausoleums were usually white or gray marble, and ranged from simple Greek Revival houses to elaborate and luxurious mansions for the dead of a wealthy family.

After a few more miles southward, James finally exited the interstate at Carrollton Avenue, and headed in the direction of the Garden District. The initial sights of modern urban life emerged. They rolled past fast food chains and grocery stores. Strip mall and auto repair eyesores dotted the landscape until finally, southwest of South Claiborne Avenue, the cold concrete melted into the warmth of wood and trees. The street became residential with small, older homes that ranged from fifty to one hundred and fifty years old, tucked away behind thick trees and bushes.

The towering levee of the Mississippi River lay aloft ahead of them at the end of Carrollton. Surely, the trolley-tracked boulevard turned a sharp, ninety-degree left onto the beautiful and historic St. Charles Avenue. Memories, nostalgia, and the warmth of familiarity rushed over Tim as they travelled the scenic street with the old-money mansions and centuries-old live oaks that created their tunneled canopy over the neutral ground. As soon as he spotted Audubon Park, he quickly turned his head to see Tulane University.

He was unable to see the newer buildings north of St. Charles, but the curb appeal of the older buildings in the front was always overwhelming. It reminded him of Yale. There was something unattainable and mysterious about Tulane. The oaks, deep green lawn, and spring flowers framed the Tudor-reminiscent architecture of the school of business and Gibson Hall perfectly.

James navigated the cumbersome SUV up the street that served as a border between Tulane and neighboring Loyola University. He continued up the narrow street whose normally full parking spaces were mostly vacant until he came to his own personalized space outside the history department building. He parked the vehicle and opened the door to step out.

James moved briskly from his SUV to the curb and up toward the entrance without a glance anywhere else. It was not a beautiful building, but not an ugly one. It was two stories of orange brick and mortar with five concrete steps that led toward the entrance. The two men passed through the white marble entranceway and into the hall.

The place smelled like the Depression Era. The tiles on the floor and the crown molding at the junction of the echo-absorbing pinhole ceiling tiles and the drywall were classic Southern Louisiana. But strangely, that was it. Everything else was quite modern.

"So this is where you work, huh?" Tim ambled with his hands in his pockets as he took in all of his surroundings.

"Yeah." James kept walking without even a look back. "It's where my office is, at least."

"Looks nice," Tim continued. "Looks new."

"That's what happens when eighty percent of the city is underwater," James said. "The water in here was a third of the way up to the ceiling. All the tile, door molding, and wall plaster had to be replaced. Really, the newer building got it worse. All that sheetrock that had to be ripped out and replaced."

"I'm ashamed to say this is the first time I've been to New Orleans since the hurricane." Tim continued to look around. "The last time was . . ."

"Here we are." James stopped at a heavy oak door about half-way down the hall and to the right.

"Your office?"

"No, not mine—the Dean of the History Department."

"Oh, shit." Tim stopped and half-jokingly fixed his tussled black hair. "Time to look respectable. Professor faces on."

James knocked before he turned the steel knob and pushed the door ajar. He hesitated. He thought Noelle had said they were in the dean's office. Maybe he had misheard. He hoped he was in the right place. *How embarrassing it would be to walk in on the dean banging a teaching assistant or something.* But he was at the point of no return. He had already lunged into the office and poked his head around the corner.

"Hello?" James announced himself with caution. "Dr. Harris?"

"James." Harris motioned him in. "Come in, come in," he smiled.

The aging man was dressed in his usual big-and-tall suit and as jovial as ever. James rarely ever saw him without a smile on his face. Each time they met, or saw one another in the hallway, Dr. Harris was always kind and cordial, well beyond common professionalism. With short gray hair that circled beneath a shiny bald head and fair, loose skin that was often pink-hued, he had the demeanor and look of someone's kindly old grandfather. He seemed a genuinely happy man in every aspect of his life. That was a rare quality in people, and James admired that.

He entered the modest-sized office with his friend in tow. The place was a mess. The bookshelves were packed tight with volumes of history texts, despite many of his books being ruined by the muddy, polluted flood waters. There were several tall, gray filing cabinets, all topped with stacks of clutter and papers. The filing cabinets were each filled to the brim, and papers of all sorts overflowed onto the shelves and desk, which no one had seen the top of in quite some time. Yet, surely Dr. Harris knew where everything was. Chaos *was* his organization. Clutter *was* his system, and some regard that as a sign of genius.

"You brought a guest," Harris said as he shook James's hand. "Dr. Broussard said you might."

James looked over at Noelle, whose grin always appeared devious and seductive. They tried to be discreet at work but people picked up on it, as did Dr. Harris. He did not mind, though others in the university frowned upon faculty relationships. Harris just hung his head a bit, almost with a blush. James also glanced in curiosity at the strange man in the office. *Who the hell is this guy?*

"Yes." James motioned to Harris. "Tim, this is Dr. Lester Harris, Dean of the History Department. Dr. Harris, this is Dr. Timothy Horn—Yale professor of Civil War History and Antebellum South."

"Dr. Horn, your reputation precedes you." He reached for Tim's hand and shook it excitedly. "I'm familiar with your work on the relationships of slaves with their masters before and during the war. A few of the professors here even use your book in the classroom."

"Thank you very much." Tim smiled courteously, and then spoke in a lowered tone to James. "I have fans."

"Book?" James responded with surprise and even agitation. "You wrote a book? I didn't know that."

"Yeah, a couple of years ago," Tim shrugged.

"Tim, I'm the majority stockholder in a textbook publishing company. Why didn't you come to me?"

"We were on the skids." Tim threw up his hands. "You didn't want to even talk to me, much less publish my book."

"But still, you could have—" James was interrupted by Noelle, who pretended to clear her throat. "Right," he said, embarrassed, and looked about the room at all the speechless onlookers. "Sorry."

"I'm Dr. Richard Conner." The stranger in the room pierced the awkwardness with a soothing, but heavy British dialect, and extended his hand to both James and Tim.

"Dr. Conner is one of the newest members of the history faculty," Harris introduced him. "He just began at the start of the spring semester. He specializes in Caribbean history and imperialism."

"A pleasure." James shook the man's hand, as did Tim. "I haven't had a chance to meet you yet."

"It takes some time to finally meet everyone," Conner replied. "At my last university, it took me two years to finally meet most of the staff in my department."

He seemed cultured, though it may have been the accent. That, to most Americans, can make nearly anyone seem well-educated and worldly. But he was a professor, and looked the part, gray and well dressed. *Yep, professorly.*

"So I'm curious," James started. "What did Dr. Broussard's team find under 'Old Hickory' in the square?"

"I'm curious too," Conner beamed as his eyes lit up. "Dr. Broussard and the dean are the only ones in the room who have seen it."

"We found this locked, rusted iron box in 'Jackson Hole.'" She almost laughed at her own joke. "We were examining the moisture in the soil and trying to figure out why such a drastic instance of subsidence happened when I came across this thing packed under a thin layer of dirt."

Harris turned to a bookshelf behind his desk, and came back a tad awkward with a beaten but solid iron box in his hand. It was roughly the size and dimensions of a cigar box and covered with rust and traces of dried soil still flaking off it.

"We had to call the custodian's office to bring some bolt cutters, but we got it opened." Harris pulled back the lid with a squeak and grind of its old hinges. "This is what we found."

James did not reach at first. He and the other two men simply stretched their necks. They formed odd expressions around their mouths as if to wail and looked down their noses into the old iron time capsule. Inside was no treasure of gold or priceless artifact, but rather an old, discolored piece of paper. Puzzlement lined his brow as he reached into the box to retrieve the old paper as Tim and Conner peered over his shoulder.

"A letter?" James examined.

"Can you read it?" Harris asked. He knew the answer and became even more excited.

"It's French," he replied, still eyeing the item in his hand. "It's an older dialect, but I should be able to." He studied it further, and slowly read aloud.

Dearest Jean Pierre,

If you are reading this letter, you have reached manhood and I sadly did not bear witness. I never thought I would have a wife and child, but you and your mother have brought me great happiness of which I am perhaps undeserving. I regret having to leave you both, and I wish I could have returned to watch you grow, but your safety was too important. Please know that I think of you every day and love you beyond words that I could ever hope to find.

Upon reaching manhood, you will receive all that I have left behind— property and fortune. It is but all I can do to right the wrong of leaving you behind. But more importantly, I charge you with a great responsibility. You will take my place as the keeper of a most important relic that must never fall into the wrong hands. It has unrivaled power and must be guarded and remain hidden. Your mother will tell you everything you need to know. Remember: Where the true king walks with the last saint of the east, the key to mankind's history resides in the very brick and mortar of the hearth where his tools are created.

Your loving father,
Jean Lafitte

"Jean Lafitte?" Wonderment struck James's face as he saw the dean become more ecstatic.

"The pirate, right?" Noelle commented. "I remember learning about him in eighth grade Louisiana history."

"More of a privateer," James corrected, as he was prone to do. "A privateer has special permission from a government, through a letter of marque, to raid the ships and settlements of competing imperial countries."

"So a pirate," she restated.

"Yeah, he would have been regarded as a pirate by the other countries' authorities," James admitted. "He was public enemy number one in U.S.-owned Louisiana."

"Can you believe it?" Harris suddenly gushed. "There is barely any official documentation of Lafitte—much of what we know is folklore. And now we find a letter written by his own hand! Oh, Tulane is going to get some national attention for this."

"And to a son," Tim added. "I wasn't aware that he had a son."

"It's thought that he did," Conner corrected. "When he died near Omoa, Honduras, the obituary in Cartagena, Colombia—that's where he had his letter of marque—stated that he was survived by a mulatto wife and an infant son named Jean Pierre," he explained as he pointed to the letter.

"But his son was supposed to have died in an eighteen thirty-two cholera outbreak here in New Orleans," Harris interjected.

"So how did this end up underneath the statue of Jackson in eighteen fifty-three?" James posed the question.

"And what is this mysterious relic mentioned in the letter?" Tim added.

No one spoke for some time. The four historians were each lost in their own thoughts, though the unspoken questions were largely the same.

"Dr. Harris, do you mind if I scanned or ran a copy of this letter?" James blurted.

"Well," Harris spoke with hesitation, "I don't know if that's a good idea. It's nearly two hundred years old and very delicate. I don't know what the Xerox machine would do to the ink or the paper."

"I understand." James nodded in disappointed acceptance.

"Just take a picture with your phone," Tim suggested.

"My phone doesn't have a camera," James stated as he turned to his friend.

"What?" Tim reeled in amazement, and perhaps a touch of appall.

"I was thinking about upgrading my phone, but my contract isn't up for a few months, so I can't get the discount." He sighed and pulled a very simple cell phone from his pocket to display it to his friend.

"You're a millionaire and you can't pony up the cash to buy a smartphone outright?" Tim continued. "It's the twenty-first century, James. You need to upgrade. You're using the same phone old Andy Jackson used to text President Madison to let him know he'd won the Battle of New Orleans." He produced a smartphone from his jacket pocket, and touched the screen a few times to open the camera function before he snapped a quick and clear shot of the letter.

"Gentlemen, will you excuse me?" Conner said as he fiddled with his own cell phone and headed for the door. "Got a text from my wife."

No one said anything. They only grinned and politely acknowledged his personal business, and then returned their attention to one another and the rare correspondence lying on the desk.

"This intrigues me, Dr. Harris," James said. "I'm going to give this some more thought. Can we get together next week sometime and discuss it more?"

"Sure thing," he replied with a smile. "I've got to get going anyway. I have a massage scheduled for a little later."

A massage? James tried to hide a bit of disgust. *I could have done without that image.*

"And we have some catching up and partying to do, don't we, Jimbo?" Tim nudged James as Noelle rolled her eyes.

Chapter 3

General P.G.T. Beauregard's sharp eyes peered downward on the study that sprawled before him, witness to the antics and conversation below. He was a looming figure—almost alive in the way he was always present and so very real. Noelle felt the need to watch the painting out of the corner of her eye as if he would creep up and tap her on the shoulder.

Two lamps in the room set the perfect ambiance and mood for the evening. They brought out the colors of the Persian rugs and pristinely upholstered eighteenth century chairs and sofas. It allowed the deeply-stained coffee tables, end tables, and crimson floorboards to be warm, soothing, and full of character. It neither washed out nor hid the deep red-and-gold nineteenth century fleur-de-lis wallpaper. It was refreshing and cozy—a perfect setting.

The aroma of a masterfully-crafted crawfish étouffée lingered in the air to fill every room in the house. The three stomachs in the home's study were also full. And they were full of alcohol. The men sipped fine bourbon whiskey intermittently with bottles of English artisan brown ale. Noelle stuck to a full-bodied Pinot Noir pulled from the sizable stash of wine in one of the courtyard cellars. Laughter resonated from wall to wall. It grew louder and heftier throughout the night as blood-alcohol content grew more toxic.

"It was one of those nights where everyone in the fraternity house got laid," Tim loudly recounted with a swing of his bourbon as he talked with his hands. "We threw this party that we literally invited Baton Rouge to. Like, eight hundred people showed. We went through thirty kegs of beer and forty coolers full of the super-strong girly punch stuff. It was insane," he recited as James grinned and Noelle beamed with yet another story about her fiancé that she had never heard.

Tells it the same way every time. And has to tell it every time. His best times.

"So anyway, our 'historian/secretary' took the title quite literally, and bought a video camera to 'document' things." He made little finger quotes as he slurred his speech. "He got his camera and took an old tradition to a higher technological level. It's called 'ledging.' When we knew somebody in the house was getting laid, a few of us would crawl out onto the ledge outside of our rooms upstairs—you know, out the window. And then we'd crawl down the ledge to the guy's room, and usually he knew we were coming. He was proud he was getting some tail, and so he didn't mind people bearing witness. So usually, he'd leave the light on. So this guy, Trent, got his camera and videotaped all of the ledging sessions. He filmed like six guys having sex that night."

"Did he record you?" she turned to James. He covered his eyes and nodded with uneasiness as his fiancée gaped with amusement.

"Jimbo, here, kicked his roommate out and got the girl up on the top bunk so everyone could see," Tim continued.

"Everyone?" Noelle asked.

"Like six or seven of us standing on the roof of this lower-level extension of the house," Tim affirmed. "And he left the window open so the camera could get sound. Jim was a legend after this. He had this girl calling him a god. Not just 'oh God!' but 'you're a god!'"

"I can attest to that," she commented as James burst with laughter and a touch of embarrassment.

"So she gets up on top of him with her back to the window, and somehow, that's when she decided to look behind her," Tim chuckled. "She sees all these guys outside watching and freaks out."

"We jumped down onto the lower bunk, out of sight of the window," James cut in. "She was going crazy, and all I could do was play dumb and act like I didn't know they were there."

"Aw." Noelle rubbed his arm. "Poor girl. I bet you had blue balls and you deserved it," she said as she patted his knee.

"Actually, I convinced her to finish up on the bottom bunk." James burst as Noelle nearly sprayed her red wine from her mouth with laughter.

The three continued to laugh as Noelle tried to catch any wine that dripped from her mouth and prevent it from staining the rare, antique furniture. "He still visits that frat house when he's in Baton Rouge; stirs up shit with the young bucks, buying them drinks and getting them into fights. Then he takes off out of there when the trouble starts," she half yelled.

"Now you guys are all settled down." Tim's smile fleeted into pseudo-seriousness. "No more fun like that for you."

"I began settling down long ago. Why don't you try it? You might like it better." James took another sip of his whiskey.

"Settle down?" he almost snarled. "I did get pretty serious with a girl a few years ago. We almost moved in together. I loved the woman."

"What happened?" Noelle inquired.

"I also love women," he stated. "I like variety. I get too used to one woman. I don't want to hurt anyone, so I don't settle in too long," he explained as he took a sip.

"But monogamy and love are beautiful things," she offered.

"To you," he rebutted. "To a woman. Men aren't like that. Some settled guys are okay with just taking a peek at a tight, younger ass or rack at the pool once in a while, but make no mistake—monogamy is not natural."

"What do you mean?" she sneered. "Of course it's natural. Why else would we do it?"

"Inheritance reasons," he explained. "It's a human-invented institution. Thousands of years ago, as civilization was born, people with trades, business, and property had to leave it all to someone one day, and unless you were monogamous there was no real way to prove an heir. There were no DNA paternity tests."

"So you're saying that monogamy is unnatural?" she scoffed.

"Yes," he exaggeratedly nodded. "It's just been around too long for most people to challenge it—kind of like religion. Males in every species of animal are hard-wired, instinctively, to mate with as many females as possible to ensure the survival of the species. It is in the DNA of every female to be selective with the male she mates with—it ensures that only the best genes get passed along. On top of that, women are more emotional and attached when it comes to sex and relationships. It's because women have to carry and raise the child. Besides, back in the day, a quarter of all women died in childbirth. So yes, they have more at stake. Men are just less attached to it, and instinctively players. Most guys just fake it as best they can. Guys like me are the few who stay truest to instinct. How can I argue with Mother Nature? Either I stay single and hurt the women I'm with at minimal levels, or I get married, cheat, and *really* hurt someone."

"Well, we'll just have to agree to disagree," she said as she gulped her wine.

The doorbell was a giant concrete dam that spontaneously popped up in the middle of a raging river. It was a mountain set down before a speeding train that violently derailed any and all trains of thought in the room. Heads jolted in the direction of the front door of the quiet French Quarter home as deep puzzlement saturated the expression on James's face.

"Did you order a pizza or something?" Tim half joked as he puzzled as well.

"What the hell? It's nine thirty." James slowly stood from his chair and set down his glass of whiskey. "You know who it might be?" The epiphany relieved him as he turned to Noelle. "The crazy old lady that lives next door."

"Oh yeah. She's sweet. This older lady next door lives alone, and she likes to walk over to her favorite bar, get hammered, and walk back only to discover that she has once again locked herself out of her house," she explained to Tim.

"Does this happen often?" Tim chuckled a bit as he stood up too.

"A couple of times a month," he said as he continued to move for the door.

"Why would she come to you?" Tim asked in wonderment.

"Well, the first time it happened, I was coming home, and she looked distraught," he explained. "She was going to call a locksmith, and she was concerned that all of the services were closed. So I told her I could pick the lock, and she's been coming to me for help ever since. She usually pays me with a beer from her fridge, and I just let her show her gratitude," James smiled.

"I think I'd find it creepier that a guy next door can pick a lock," Tim commented, and then sped his step to follow James. "Hold on, I've gotta see this."

James cautiously opened his front door. He feared that, in these more turbulent times, the visitor may not be the harmless lady next door. Indeed, upon opening the door, James did not find a sweet, drunk, older lady on his porch, but it was not a home invader either. Instead, it was an older man, perhaps in his fifties. He was well dressed in a more casual beige suit, and combined with a full head of gray hair and gentle smile, he exuded astuteness and class.

"Yes? Can I help you?" James stood with the door half open, Tim leering over his shoulder a few feet behind.

"Pardon my intrusion." The stranger smiled with his heavy British accent. "I know it's late, and I debated whether to come tonight or just wait for morning, but I wanted to be sure to catch you at home, Dr. Beauregard."

"And you are?" James was a bit surprised that the man knew his name.

"Oh, please excuse me," he said as he grasped James's cautious hand. "I'm Dr. Rylan Reed. I'm a professor at Oxford."

"Hey, I know this guy." Tim stepped up with a smile and nudged his way into the doorway. "He hosts a BBC show about off-beat alternative history. He investigates other historical possibilities about things that there isn't a lot of record on—William Wallace, King Arthur, Robin Hood. I especially liked the one on Atlantis. It's called . . ." Tim struggled to recall the name of the show.

"*What if* . . ." Reed provided the elusive title. "I wasn't aware that you would know it. It's not quite as interesting as your American reality programs," he smiled.

"Oh yeah." James's face relaxed. "I haven't seen the show, but I've seen you as a contributor on The History Channel. Please, come in." He stepped aside to allow the grateful man to enter the warmth of the old house from the chill in the March air.

"Beautiful home." Reed gazed around in exaggeration at the nineteenth century house. "I love the color of the floors." He motioned to the crimson boards.

"They have a story all their own," James spoke as he led the man inside. "Would you care for a drink? Bourbon? Beer? Wine?"

"Would you happen to have a scotch?" he inquired politely.

"Eighteen-year-old MacAllen okay?"

"Perfect." Reed followed into the study and introduced himself to Noelle. "Hello. How do you do? Rylan Reed." He shook her hand lightly as she introduced herself.

James stumbled a bit on his way to the minibar set up near his desk. His hand was shaky and less coordinated than normal. He rattled the crystal decanter and some fine glassware as he opened the fine scotch and took a sniff. He savored its unique aroma before he poured it over an ice-prepared rocks glass. His technique was sloppy, causing a bit to drip and spill. *Geez, the bourbon's taking its toll.* He displayed it in his gait while he waltzed comfortably toward his guest to deliver the drink.

"Thank you," Reed said, accepted the glass. "Cheers," he toasted as everyone sipped their own spirits.

"So, at the expense of seeming rude, what are you doing here?" James plopped into his chair.

"Oh no," he began to apologize. "I'm rude for visiting at this hour. I'm sorry I didn't have your telephone number, so I couldn't contact you to announce myself. I'm visiting New Orleans on holiday—I do at least once a year because I love the food and culture. I called Dr. Harris who is a dear friend of mine. He told me about this wonderful discovery in Jackson Square, but alas, he was not available to let me see the letter."

"You're here over the Lafitte letter?" Tim puzzled.

"My specialty at Oxford is British military history," he explained. "I especially deal with the Napoleonic and nineteenth century imperial era, including the war with the United States at that time."

"The War of 1812," Noelle said.

"Precisely," Reed continued. "And since the Battle of New Orleans was a major engagement, I naturally know all about Jean Lafitte and the Barataria corsairs and their exploits."

"And so Dr. Harris must have told you we took a picture, and you want to see," James said. "Sure, why not? Anything for a colleague. Tim, can you sync your phone up with my printer?"

"I could send it to your e-mail and let you print." He thumbed through his electronic images until he located the picture of the letter. "Okay . . . and sent. Check your e-mail, Jimbo."

"Okay, got it." James had already logged into his e-mail. "Printing . . ."

The high definition laser printer upon James's expansive oak desk sprang to life in an abrupt and almost startling manner. The cartridge track clicked and then briefly halted with the surge of power and information. LED lights ignited and then the cartridges moved horizontally with a robotic sound.

"Here, take a look." James circled from around his desk and handed it to the seated Dr. Reed. "Can you read French?"

"Sure." His gaze never left the page.

He carefully studied the printout of the Lafitte letter. He was entranced, his eyes moving from side to side with each line of looped, almost calligraphic handwritten text. He read it slowly in order to interpret the French to English as his lips moved with each word.

"My God." Reed removed his reading glasses after several minutes and set the paper onto the coffee table. "Quite astounding, don't you think?" He smiled giddily at the others in the room.

"Sure," James agreed. "Jean Lafitte is an almost mythical figure. There isn't much documentation on him, and to find a letter written supposedly by him personally is pretty cool."

"Pretty cool?" Reed smiled. "This is more than pretty cool. This cryptic language and mention of items of immense value? There's something to this."

"What?" James nearly scoffed at the idea. "Like buried treasure?

People have been looking for his buried treasure since he died, and no one ever found any. He's a cult figure. People didn't even believe he was dead for decades—they had to launch an investigation to assure people of that. He was the nineteenth century equivalent of Elvis or Tupac."

"I don't know, Jimbo," Tim interjected. "You have to admit that the mention of an item that should not fall into the wrong hands, coupled with where the letter was found is pretty strange."

"That's exactly what I was thinking," Noelle added. "This letter was to be entrusted to Lafitte's son upon reaching manhood. Why wasn't it passed down within the family? Why wasn't it found in a coffee can in some old lady's attic? Instead of it turning up on *Antiques Roadshow*, it was found hidden under the statue of Jackson."

"Jean-Pierre Lafitte died of Cholera in eighteen thirty-two, when he was about eleven, and probably his mother, too," James argued. "What family would it have been passed down within?"

"Exactly," Reed blurted. "If it turned up beneath a statue set in place in eighteen fifty-three and Jean-Pierre died over twenty years before, who would have placed it there? Obviously someone who knew this secret—someone else trusted by the elder Jean."

"Maybe one of Lafitte's other crew members?" Noelle suggested.

"Yeah, Lafitte had other captains that reported to him," Tim agreed. "They all worked out of Barataria. Maybe one of them was a plan B."

"I don't think so." James shook his head, now deep in thought over what they suggested about buried treasure. "No honor among thieves. These are pirates we're talking about."

"Privateers," Noelle corrected with a smile.

"Same difference," he shot back. "Smartass. Either way, they were all out to advance themselves. Even the other captains would have likely taken the booty for themselves if they had half a chance."

"Okay," Noelle redirected. "Still, we're back at square one. Who put the box under Jackson's statue?"

"Perhaps if we follow the clues, that may be answered," Reed suggested.

James and Tim sat in the chairs they had occupied all evening. No one spoke. They stared into space or scanned the room for some item that may aid their thought processes. They sipped their whiskey or wine, and searched in vain for a miraculous epiphany.

"Where the true king walks with the last saint of the east," James spoke aloud, but almost to himself, his thoughts verbalized as he brought the glass of whiskey to his mouth.

But rather than allow the fiery liquid to touch his lips, he instead directed his gaze into the glass, and then moved it slowly away from his face. He narrowed his brow for a moment, and then it relaxed in happiness. He smiled and jumped from his seat to head for the minibar while the others in the room watched him in curiosity. He picked up a half empty bottle from the top of the bar, and then walked briskly back to the coffee table to set it down before them with a pop.

"Who would the 'true king' be to a Frenchman in the eighteen twenties?" he asked.

"Well, Napoleon eventually replaced Louis XVI." Reed searched his memory.

"And while Napoleon was exiled, Louis XVIII ruled briefly—the monarchy reinstated," Tim added.

But while James smiled and the two history professors recounted French Revolution history, they each searched the bottle that was set before them. Then they both saw, in plain, bold letters, what James wanted to show them.

"Bourbon," they spoke in unison, as if they came to the same conclusion at once.

"Napoleon replaced the Bourbon royal family after the Revolution—the true kings of France!" Reed stated.

James had already leapt from his seat to head back toward his desk. He rounded the side and stood facing the wall behind it. He brought his finger to the surface of a framed replica of an old map of New Orleans with the French Quarter in the center. He traced a line down Bourbon Street from west to east as he whispered the cross streets along the way.

"Saint Louis, Saint Peter, Saint Anne, Saint Phillip . . ." He smiled, and then turned with a laugh. "The last saint-named street that crosses Bourbon on the east end of the street is Saint Phillip. Do you know what's at Bourbon and Saint Phillip?"

"Oh my God," Tim uttered with a smile as he buried his face in his hands. "Lafitte's Blacksmith Shop."

"His New Orleans smuggling headquarters." Reed was astonished.

"And you know what it still has there?" James waited but with no reply. "A hearth of brick and mortar."

"Where man's tools are created," Reed finished the sentence from the letter as he beamed.

Noelle had already picked up her smartphone and giddily opened her home screen. As her favorite search engine loaded, she clicked the search field, and typed the key words that she needed.

"There she goes." James stepped aside with a chuckle. "The Google Queen. The most minute, insignificant factoid could enter her ear, and she's already searching," he explained while she shot him playful dirty looks.

A couple of minutes passed while she flew through the pages that resulted. She refined the search as she needed, and tapped on various pages that contained something like the description she was looking for.

"Okay." She finally spoke, still surfing her search results as she relayed the information she had gathered at that point. "Lafitte's Blacksmith Shop was around at least by the seventeen seventies, and some believe it dates to as early as the seventeen twenties, built by a man named Nicolas Touze."

"Probably not a lot of surviving records that go that far back," Tim commented. "I'm sure the fire in seventeen eighty-eight destroyed them along with the original Cabildo building."

"Yes," she continued with her eyes fixed to the screen. "But neither that one, nor the one in seventeen ninety-four destroyed the blacksmith shop. Ownership of it is pretty vague before the eighteen thirties. There is record of a transfer of ownership in eighteen thirty-two to a man named Pierre Lafleur, and then various owners until now."

"The same year that the son died of cholera," Reed commented. "What do we know about him? Was he perhaps a crew member of Lafitte's?"

"Doesn't say. But I guess records wouldn't indicate whether the man was a known public enemy. What's interesting is that there's nothing that says whether or not it was sold to Lafleur privately or if it was an auction held by the city—it's just a record of transfer."

"Very strange," Reed uttered as he became even more excited. "To think that there may be some sort of treasure just a few blocks away, and in a bar, no less."

"There's only one way to find out," Tim said with a devious grin. "What do you think, Jim? Ready to go out on the town?"

"Well. You've been wanting to hit Bourbon Street. It's just not the titty end of the street. Up for it, baby?" He turned to Noelle for approval.

"Oh no," she waved him off with a grin. "I've had my share of adventures with you. You boys have fun. I'm going to research this Pierre Lafleur guy."

"Dr. Reed?" James turned to the aging British professor. "What do you say?"

"Just allow me to use your loo, and I'll be right with you gentlemen," he smiled as he stood up.

"Around the corner and left down the hall," James said as he pointed and then watched the excited older man disappear. "Treasure hunting it is, then," he toasted, and swilled back the rest of his bourbon.

Chapter 4

Saint Phillip Street was darker and quieter than the rest of the district, even during spring break. While the western side of the French Quarter bustled with traffic and drunken college students, the eastern side was docile in comparison. By day, shops, hotels, and restaurants drew moderate levels of older clientele who strolled the narrow streets with admiration of the Spanish-style cast iron galleries and tropical hanging plants affront old Greek Revival buildings. They dined on fine Creole cuisine and browsed art galleries and higher-end souvenirs.

By night, the iron galleries were tastefully lit as people frequented their favorite low-key pubs and taverns. But it was a far cry from the other end of the Quarter. There were no gaudy neon signs luring the drunken hordes into clubs and hazy strip bars. There were no cups or cans in beer-filled gutters. There was no stale smell of urine and alcohol on the humid night air. Hip-hop, jazz, and zydeco did not blare from open doors to wage battle for supremacy amongst coeds ready to disrobe for a cheap set of plastic beads.

"I love New Orleans." Dr. Reed took in the sights as the three professors strode northward toward Bourbon Street. "Am I even saying that right?"

"Well, a lot of people say *NWahlins*," James corrected.

"Or even just *Nawlins*," Tim added.

"So you've been here a few times?" James asked.

"Many times. I usually try to make it down here at least once a year."

"Wow. From England? Business or pleasure?"

"Usually on holiday," Reed said. "I'm divorced and my son just turned thirty-one, so I have no one to answer to. As I said, I love this city. And there's why." He gestured ahead.

Saint Phillip opened to Bourbon Street as a river into a bay, which was slightly heavier with foot traffic, but nothing like the crowds at the Canal Street end. There, on the opposite left corner stood a building that appeared as an old man surrounded by his grandchildren. Most of the buildings near the corner were two-story Greek Revival homes, some now converted to retail space. They ranged in age from the eighteen twenties to much younger one-story Victorian homes with porches that featured ornate looped molding at the angles between the posts and roof beams.

But the old man was Lafitte's Blacksmith Shop. It was one of the oldest buildings in the city; a true example of what all of New Orleans might have looked like in the eighteenth century. The old French colonial-style cottage's pitched roof was complete with three upper windows, and sat perched upon exposed wooden beams and brick walls with the stucco chipped away in some areas. It was rustic, yet fully restored in its authentic state. Inside, one could have a quiet drink and be transported to another era that burst with culture. Lafitte's was not for the average New Orleans reveler—it was for the connoisseur.

The three men marveled for a moment, though the building was not something new to them, and then stepped toward it, time travelling between eras. They walked from eighteen twenties Greek Revival homes and crossed twentieth century pavement. They then stepped up onto the opposite curb, transported again into the eighteenth century period, and entered through the French doors into the smoky, dimly-lit bar.

Even during spring break, it was a dead Monday night. The interior was typically dark, the only light emanating from the gas lights outside, from the flickering votive candles on the tabletops, and from the small television above the bar with an earlier broadcast of the day's top story— the sinking of Jackson's statue. Most of the tables were empty, except for an older man and his wife who sipped cocktails at one of the tables closer to the entrance. Original wooden beams overhead were exposed, fixed with slowly churning ceiling fans.

Behind the bar was a multi-leveled shelf space lined with various liquors. The bar area was cluttered and small. Glassware and minimal back counter space fought for supremacy with the bulky, outdated cash register. T-shirts, tank tops, and children's apparel hung along the back wall for purchase. The solitary barmaid darted from one end to the other, cleaning a few glasses and keeping things stocked in an effort to combat boredom.

"Hi, guys," she greeted less than enthusiastically as she spotted the three gentlemen enter the bar. She smiled lazily, her dark, mysterious brown eyes barely open. She threw her very long, dark tresses over the back of her tank top-clad shoulders to expose her slender physique, several ear and nose piercings, and blue butterfly tattoo on her right arm.

"Hi." Tim smiled with obvious admiration of her attributes.

"Go get her, tiger," James mocked. "And get us a couple of drinks," he continued in a whisper. "You guys try to keep her distracted. I'm going to go check out the hearth."

Reed and Tim veered and headed to the bar while James continued to the left. He eyed the original blacksmith's hearth in the center of the room, located directly across from the bar area. It was in the condition it would have been in Lafitte's time and before, a crude brown brick fireplace with a chimney that reached up and through the roof. The wide base, complete with a mantle, featured a double-sided pit. The second tier continued upward to the chimney. He circled the centerpiece structure with reverence and awe given the newfound allegations of what may lie hidden inside. He examined, first, from afar to see if there were any indications as to where some kind of compartment may be.

"What can I get for you guys?" the petite bartender asked in a deeper female voice that was unexpected from such a small body.

"Bourbon," Tim replied. He bellied up and then pointed to Reed. "Scotch."

"And let me guess, a beer for your friend over there?" She grinned in an attempt at a George Thorogood joke.

"Um, another bourbon, actually," Tim said as she reached for glasses, filled them with ice, and grabbed bottles from the shelf behind her. "And your number," he wooed with his most alluring, seductive smile.

"Eighteen, Prince Charming. Eighteen dollars," she said, and rolled her eyes as she slid the drinks across the bar and walked away.

"What?" He turned to Reed as he removed his wallet and then a credit card. "I'm very charming. I'm a very charming Yale professor. Cultured and—"

"It takes a lot more than that to get into these . . . well, I'm not wearing panties," she said.

"You have a lot to learn about women, my young friend." Reed's astute British accent dripped from his every word.

"Oh, you're English." Her eyes lit up as she pushed down his way, leaned over the bar, and smiled, her chin propped up on her hand.

"I'm going to go check on Jim," Tim said as he rolled his eyes and carried the two drinks around the corner.

He crossed the wooden floors of the space between the bar and the blacksmith's hearth, careful not to spill the two drinks as he stepped with a bit of intoxication. James still circled like a scavenger bird, periodically grasping bricks in an attempt to test for some sort of looseness.

"Thanks." James took the bourbon from Tim's hand. "What happened, Don Juan?" He looked toward the bar to see that the girl behind chatted attentively with Dr. Reed.

"Apparently, she prefers the superficial things like stupid British accents," Tim scoffed.

"As opposed to superficial things like being a Yale professor?"

"Ha, ha," Tim feigned amusement. "Find anything?"

"No. It's too damned dark to see anything."

"There's an app for that." Tim removed his smartphone from his jacket pocket, and flipped through his applications before he pressed the touch-screen to bring up an image of a flashlight. Upon pressing the power button on the flashlight, the camera's flash illuminated as he scanned every inch of the hearth for anything unusual.

"Hey, look at this, Jimbo." He stopped to shine the light on a brick three levels down and at the center of the lower hearth. "This mortar is lighter-colored than the rest."

"I see that." James crouched down for a closer look. "And there's a bit of dried mortar on the front edges of the brick like it's been replaced or repaired."

"You think that's what we're looking for?"

"Only one way to find out."

James set out in search of anything that he might use as a tool. He checked frequently to make sure Dr. Reed kept the bartender occupied. He saw nothing at first, but then he caught sight of something in the back near the bathrooms. With a grin, he bolted in that direction. He picked up a couple of items from the back wall near the floor and returned with a flat-head screwdriver and a small but heavy pipe wrench.

"You know these old bars," James said as he returned. "Always having bathroom issues."

He once again crouched before the hearth and then knelt down like a worshipper as Tim kept light on the brick. James located the area they had spotted before, and ran his fingers over the edges of the mortar before he placed the sharp end of the screwdriver into part of the seam. He then struck the handle with the wrench, and paused to make sure it didn't make too much noise. But it held no contest to the jukebox and the classic rock song it blared, so he continued to strike, finally with a crack along the mortar line. Encouraged, he chipped away until the brick loosened and shifted around between the others.

James looked up at his friend's shock and beamed with excitement. He returned his attention to the darkly-colored brick, and grasped what he could of the slightly protruded edge and worked it back and forth until it finally slid from its position.

"Shine the light in there," he told his friend as he laid the brick on the thin pile of mortar chippings that dusted the floor.

"Jim, there's no brick behind this one," Tim gaped as he lowered the light to shine into the hole. "Reach in there and see."

James was apprehensive. Dark, dank places made him nervous, for amongst his many fears, spiders were his least favorite things on the earth. South Louisiana was no stranger to highly venomous arachnids—black widows and brown recluses being the worst. The light did not penetrate very deeply into the void, but as far as he could tell, there were no milky funnel webs. He slowly lifted his hand to the hole, and inched inside to probe deeper and deeper into the hearth.

"Oh shit," James suddenly exclaimed, which startled his friend.

"What? What?"

"I've got something." James retracted his hand to reveal yellowish aged paper scrolled and tied with a red ribbon.

He handed the rolled paper to Tim, and then carefully replaced the brick in hopes that no one would notice the damage before it was time to leave. He then stood up and walked over to one of the tables in the back of the room to rejoin his friend already seated. James carefully pulled the ribbon and unrolled the sheets to lay them flat on the table. They were medium-sized sheets of faded paper, all with quill-written text.

"Looks like the same handwriting from the letter." Tim used his phone flashlight to get a better look.

"And judging by where this was found, I'm going to guess that this *is*, in fact, Lafitte's handwriting," James added. "They look like diary pages."

"Little girls have diaries, Jim," Tim said with sarcasm. "Pirates have journals. Logs? Not diaries."

"Okay." He rolled his eyes. "Journal pages. See the uneven tearing on the left side of the pages?"

"Did you find anything?" Reed's accent found their ears. "Dear God, you did." He sat down and glared at the pages.

"Certainly not buried treasure," James said, keeping his eyes on their find. "Looks like three pages from Lafitte's journal. The first is dated July 21, 1811. The second is September 4, 1814. And the last is from March 2, 1817."

"That's odd," Reed commented. "Where's the rest of the journal? Why tear out these specific pages?"

"He obviously didn't want anyone finding these particular ones," Tim replied. "Hence, they're hidden in the hearth. He did say in the letter to Jean-Pierre that he was entrusting him with an item that can't fall into the wrong hands." He turned his attention to James. "What do the pages say?"

"Let's see." James began reading to himself at first. "He raided a British ship named the *HMS Danbury* three days before, somewhere off the coast of Pensacola, Florida. He lost two men in looting the captain's quarters where his men found a small chest that contained a stone jaguar figurine and a page from a Spanish captain's log dated 1809."

James translated silently before reading aloud. "*One of my crew members is from Guatemala. He seemed afraid of the figurine, for he would scarcely come near it. I had him translate the captain's log. It documents the plundering of a small village in Guatemala. The inhabitants claim to be the guardians of a great city of the gods. They were slaughtered and their prized possession—the figurine—was stolen. There is also a set of sketches at the bottom of the page, drawn from some kind of tall, stone totem in the village. My crewman recognized it. He says it refers to the jaguar as the guardian and key to a great temple of the rising sun, where man may ask the gods to change his life. Since the figurine has been on my ship, I've had dreams each night in which a great jaguar prowls the jungle after me. My crewman says the jaguar chooses its own master.*"

"Strange," Reed said as he shook his head.

"So wait," Tim offered. "We're not looking for buried gold? The treasure is a stupid stone figurine?"

"Even if it is," Reed said, almost offended, "it would still be an important archaeological find. Read the next one."

"Okay, this is the one from September of 1814," James began. "*I was visited by two British commanders this evening. I suppose I should have seen this coming, but they plan to attack the port of New Orleans soon. They have offered me letters of marque and estates in England in return for aiding them in naval support against the Americans. But it is even more intriguing that they also sought to recover the stone jaguar plundered from one of their ships some years ago. They claim their king would pay handsomely for it, so it must be of great value to them. Between their interest in it and my dreams of the jaguar in the jungle, I am convinced of its power. I cannot let it be taken by the British. I believe the Americans will prevail in this war. Perhaps I can bargain with Governor Claiborne and offer my assistance against the British in return for the release of my brother. Perhaps I can entrust the jaguar to the Americans."*

"I'm quite familiar with this one," Reed informed the others. "Captains McWilliams and Lockyer approached Lafitte under a white flag to negotiate for his aid against the Americans, and if he refused they would destroy Barataria."

"Instead, the Americans destroyed Barataria," James interrupted. "And still Lafitte aided the Americans. Why?"

"The release of his brother Pierre," Tim offered. "Plain and simple. Everyone knows he disappeared from prison just after the pirates helped defend the city."

"But after the raid and destruction of Barataria?" James argued. "I don't know. It says here in Lafitte's own handwriting that he sought to entrust the jaguar, and whatever power he's talking about, to the Americans. Somehow he trusts them over the British. What was he afraid the British were going to do? He apparently feared them gaining it."

He shuffled the page behind the other two, ready to read the last by the light of Tim's cell phone flashlight when a sharp, electronic sound chimed through the smoky, music-filled space. James was always self-conscious about his ringtone when around others. He only wanted it to stop. He dug furiously within his jeans pocket to find the device. He finally removed it, pressed the SEND button, and lifted it to his ear.

"Hey babe, you find something?" he asked.

"Interesting shit," she said excitedly from behind the computer at home.

"Let me put you on speakerphone," he said. He pressed another button and laid the phone on the table. "Sorry about the noise. Go ahead."

"Okay," she began, competing with the bar. "I did some digging through all kinds of census and immigration records from back then, as well as property reports and such. The oldest census record of Pierre Lafleur is eighteen forty. We know the same man came to own the blacksmith shop in eighteen thirty-two. From there, it looks like he was married, and then in the eighteen fifty census he had one son, but had lost his wife. I also found record that his only child, a son named Jean-Baptiste Lafleur died in eighteen fifty-two of unknown causes."

"So in the end, he had no wife or kids that survived him," Tim clarified. "That means no one to leave the blacksmith shop to."

"Right," she said. "When he died in eighteen seventy-eight, the blacksmith shop was auctioned by the city."

"None of that is really out of the ordinary," James noted.

"But get this," she continued. "There are no birth records of this Pierre Lafleur—anyone by that name was a different person, and are all accounted for. And there are no immigration records for this guy, either. It's like he just appeared out of thin air."

"The same year Lafitte's son dies," Reed gushed with disbelief. "That's when he first appears. What if Jean-Pierre's mother helped him fake his death? Renaming him Pierre wouldn't be that big of a change, but it would be big enough. He lives the rest of his life as Pierre Lafleur, and with his only son dead by eighteen fifty-three, he hides the letter so no one could find it."

"But why?" James puzzled. "Why would an eleven- or twelve-year-old need to fake his own death? Was he in some sort of danger?"

"The letter did say the item in question could not fall into the wrong hands," Tim added. "But whose hands?"

"Read on," Reed urged. "Maybe there's something in the last page."

"Okay, guys," Noelle said. "I'm going to go to bed. You boys have fun."

"Okay, love you." James hung up the phone and picked up the last journal page. "Here goes—March 2, 1817 . . ."

"*It seems I can trust no one. The Americans are unworthy to be the keepers of such power. I still have the dreams. It has not chosen a new master. The Americans, I fear, are as greedy as the British. I feel hunted. I frequently see small British ships patrolling the coasts, though they have lost supremacy here. In New Orleans, I have thwarted several attempts on my life. Each assassin who has uttered a word has spoken like an Englishman, and some have even demanded the location of the jaguar. Mexico is in revolt. My brother and I have been given letters of marque from Spain. We have agreed to also act as spies at the revolutionary stronghold of Galveston Island. Pierre will stay here to maintain the smuggling operation in New Orleans, and I will go there to Galveston. The Spanish, to my knowledge, do not know I possess the figurine. Perhaps I will take it with me."*

"There it is," Tim exclaimed. "It's in Galveston. Why didn't we think of that before?"

"Drunk," admitted James. "It's common knowledge he set up a colony there. He basically drove out the revolutionaries and set up a similar operation to what he had going in Barataria."

"But what if it's no longer there?" Reed posed the question. "What if he took it with him when he left Galveston for Central America near the end of his life?"

"I don't think so." James sipped his bourbon. "He took his wife and infant son with him, and later sent them to New Orleans. He had to have sent the letter with the wife to be presented to Jean-Pierre in adulthood. Why would he do that if the jaguar was in Central America with him? And there's no record of him ever going back to Galveston. Maybe he hid it there forever, where no one would look for it."

"You don't think the British would have gone there looking for it after he left?" Tim asked.

"His colony was destroyed by hurricane and flooding," James argued. "Most of the colony and buildings were burned before he left."

"And now we know a possible reason why Jean-Pierre's mother faked their deaths," Reed said with excitement. "It seems that the people who were after Lafitte, driving him away to Galveston, may have been after his only son as well."

"That's some serious resolve," James said, and then thought in silence for several moments. "That means whoever these Englishmen looking for the jaguar are; they are hell-bent on getting it."

"And the people involved span across multiple generations," Tim said.

"Okay, let's get out of here." James carefully rolled the fragile old papers in the way he had found them, and tied them again with the same ribbon before he placed them loosely in his jacket pocket. "Let's go back home and talk about this some more." He stood, along with Dr. Reed, and then gulped the last of his now watered-down bourbon.

"I've got to take a piss," Tim grunted as he finished his drink as well, and moved for the restroom in the back.

"All right, we'll meet you out front," James called out as he and Dr. Reed started for the French doors they had entered through.

"Later," the bartender cooed, and waved at Dr. Reed as they exited. "Call me."

"You got her number?" James grinned at his older counterpart as he just shrugged devilishly. "You old hound dog. You're like a British man-cougar."

The two professors stepped from the stale air of the darkened bar and into the cool, moisture-laden breezes of the New Orleans night air. It was as if being transported into Lafitte's time. Aside from the distant cheers of admirers of some coed's breasts, they could faintly hear a mule-drawn carriage as it moved down one of the streets. Hooves clopped at the modern asphalt in a slow, steady rhythm that echoed from one side of the narrow old streets to the other. Above the corner where they stood, a gas-lit sconce flickered from the side of the old blacksmith shop the way it might have in another age.

"Ah," Reed sighed as he took it all in, "I love this city."

"Yeah, you and me both."

"Do you happen to have a light?" a strong Londoner's voice came from behind them down the St. Phillip side of the blacksmith shop.

The two men turned to peer down the darker street away from tourists. A man in his forties stood along the sidewalk. His hair was very short and receding. He pulled a cigarette from the paper pack in his hand and lifted it to his lips as he eyed James for a response.

"Sure," James said as he and Reed began toward him. James squinted in the darkness. *I think I know this . . . nah. Too dark. I can't tell if it's him. I better not ask.*

"Thank you," the man said as James pulled a Zippo lighter from his pocket, opened it, lit the smoke for the man, and then closed it with a sharp, metallic clink.

"Don't mention it," James said as the man began toward Bourbon Street.

He then swung around, his back to any tourists on Bourbon, catching the two professors off-guard. He brandished a solid black semi-automatic pistol from his hoodie pocket. James and Reed froze in terror at the sight of the weapon, unsure of what they were to do.

"The papers," the stranger said. "Give me the papers."

"Papers? What papers?" James replied, sure that this man could not have known about what they had just discovered inside.

"The papers from the hearth inside," he replied calmly. "Give them to me now."

"Fuck you," James said defiantly, perhaps more confidant and defiant than usual with a belly full of whiskey.

"James, maybe you should do as he—" Reed shivered, but stopped as he caught sight of something else.

From above the gunman's head, an empty brown beer bottle descended, and crashed over the man's crown. The bottle shattered in all directions across the sidewalk and pavement with little clinks of sound. Tim stood behind the man, his breathing labored with adrenaline. He looked up at James and Reed with rage in his eyes as he finally tossed aside the remainder of the bottle's neck.

"Jesus," Tim said. "You always see that shit in movies, but you never expect you'd do it in real life." He looked down at the unconscious man on the sidewalk. "What kind of shit did you get yourself into?"

James crouched to the ground over the unconscious fellow, all the while his adrenal glands commanded him to run for his life. He placed a hand on the man's shoulder, and flipped him enough to get a closer look at his face. James did recognize him. Confused, and feeling somewhat violated, he obeyed the wishes of his most primitive survival instinct.

"Come on." James rushed toward Bourbon Street, followed by his two friends. "I knew I recognized that guy. Tim, you remember? Dr. Conner, from the dean's office."

"Why the hell was he mugging you?" Tim responded, a bit winded. "You don't think he figured out what we did, do you?"

They turned the corner, intensely aware of all of their surroundings. James scanned for signs that there might have been an accomplice with Connor. He scanned every face and every tourist on the street as the three of them walked hurriedly toward the Canal Street end, and toward the party that commenced at that very moment.

"Come on," James puffed. "We'll lose whoever else might have been with this guy in the crowds."

"What the hell is going on?" Tim followed in confusion.

"That man demanded the journal pages from inside the hearth," Reed recounted.

"And he was English," James added.

"Like Lafitte described," Tim gaped. "Holy shit. This is weird. Same people?"

"Looks like it." James pulled his phone from his pocket, dialed, and pressed it to his ear. "Noelle? Yeah, it's not safe for you at the house. Pack a bag—it's okay. We're okay. Just please do as I say, and I'll explain later. Pack a bag and meet me at the Ritz on Iberville. Okay, love you." He ended the call with the push of a button and replaced the phone in his pocket.

"Looks like this shit goes deeper than we thought," Tim noted as they slowed into the crowds of the debauchery end of Bourbon. "What now?"

"We'll go back for your bags in the morning," he replied. "Then we're going to Galveston."

Chapter 5

"I said I was sorry, baby," James graveled from across the white table-cloth covered with various brunch paraphernalia. "How many times do you want me to say it?"

Tim chuckled quietly as he attempted to hide his smile beneath the back of his hand, which clutched a half-eaten English muffin. He happily played the spectator, a mere observer of a marital spat between two people who were not even married yet. That was the problem with living with someone before marriage. The two people involved practically become married just by proximity. They share responsibilities and chores. They argue over not taking out the trash or cleaning up after oneself. By the time the rings find their way onto the fingers, the couple might very well be sick of one another.

The dining room of the Ritz was quite lavish. Tables draped with fine, bright white linen lay topped with all of the polished utensils and porcelain coffee accessories needed for a beautiful New Orleans champagne brunch. Heavenly smells coursed on the air. The classic American aromas of bacon and eggs mingled with that of Creole seasonings atop roast Cornish Hen. Moist hash browns garnished with sautéed onions and julienne red bell peppers warmed in silvery chaffing dishes powered by Sterno canisters underneath. A chef tossed omelets before a mob of interested patrons and used anything from the traditional cheese and ham to boiled shrimp and crawfish.

"At least a dozen more times," Noelle fumed with another sip of her mimosa. "I had to get up in the middle of the night, scared out of my mind, and check into a hotel for four hundred dollars a night."

"I can afford it. It's not a problem," James countered.

"The money isn't the issue," she practically yelled in a silent and civil sort of way. "It's that I was scared and had to uproot, and I think you're being very insensitive to that. I forgot to even get my makeup, for Christ's sake. I look like hell."

"You look beautiful." His compliment did not seem to help. He took a bite of a bagel with strawberry cream cheese and washed it down with some rich local coffee.

"You're so focused on being young—reliving the glory days," she jeered as her eyes brought Tim into things. "You two get together and you're like frat boys again. Why don't you grow up? What the hell did you guys get yourselves into last night?"

"Apparently Jean Lafitte's dirty laundry," Tim said.

"Yeah, we basically experienced something that Lafitte described in his journal," James added. "Some guy with a British accent just showed up, pointed a gun at Reed and me, and demanded the journal pages."

"Which no one should have known about," Tim smacked as he chewed more of his muffin. "We were really the only people in the bar. And nobody could have known we were there or why we were there."

"It was Connor, Noelle. Dr. Connor. The guy from the dean's office. Remember? He was there when we were checking out the original Lafitte letter," James said somberly.

"Oh my God," she gasped. "Why would he rob you at gun point for the new pages? Is he some kind of obsessed collector or something?"

"No clue," James said with a shrug. "But it bothered me that if somebody found us there and knew what we were doing, they might be able to find out that we live just a few blocks away," James explained. "So I sent you here."

"Okay," she nodded in acceptance. "You were just looking out for us. There's no way you could have known what you were getting into. But what now? Call the cops? Get them to sit out in front of the house in a cruiser?"

"I think we have to see this through," James said, and grasped her hand.

"And what does that mean?" she shot back with the elevation of her right brow into an arch.

"We have to go to Galveston today." He cringed in his reply, the backlash pending. "We're going to go back to the house for a few things, meet Reed there, and head out."

"What?" She let go of his hand. "Aren't you done with chases and danger? This isn't Hollywood—you could get killed or something." She looked over at Tim with suspicious eyes. "Or is this a ploy to go party with college girls at the beach?"

"Hey." Tim threw up his hands in innocence. "I'm just along for the ride. No blondes in bikinis involved."

"All right, fine," she shrugged, still unhappy. "Whatever. I'm going to drive up to Baton Rouge to see my mother. I'll just stay there the rest of the week. You boys have fun, and be careful."

"We will." James jumped up with a big, gleaming smile, and dropped his white napkin on the table. "I love you. I'll call you when we get there." He rounded the table and kissed Noelle's reluctant cheek.

James turned and made his way between well-funded tourists in the dining room, and then followed the brunch buffet to the exit as Tim trailed close behind. He could not wait to get back to his own house. He needed a shower and a change of clothes. His professor-casual attire reeked with yesterday's body grime and the smell of bar smoke, which was infinitely stronger than the fumes absorbed from his own habit.

"She didn't seem too happy," Tim said as they pushed into the still cool March air.

"Oh, she'll get over it," James said as he turned right down Iberville Street toward Bourbon. "That's the thing with relationships. People fail when they try to make the other person happy all the time. Sometimes you have to do for you, and if they love you, they'll get over the petty shit. You have to make yourself happy, and so does she. And then you're just happy together. But if you set a precedence of perfection, when you dip below, you set yourself up for failure. Expectations are the enemy. Just live for the moment."

"Believe me—I know," Tim said. "I don't even try to convince a woman I'm husband material. Your expectations of me don't go beyond the bed."

After a short distance, the two of them reached Bourbon Street and made a left in the direction of the residential section of the Quarter. But first, they had to navigate the party epicenter of New Orleans. The bars, clubs, and daiquiri shops were already open, as if they never closed in the first place. The doors had reopened as late morning employees tried to scrub the previous night's funk from the walls and floors before the college students came back.

"Jesus, I don't remember all this crap." Tim stepped over various pieces of beads, cups, and condom wrappers as he navigated down the street.

"We were never awake yet. We always slept until two in the afternoon, and by then, all this was already cleaned up. Well, most of it. You get a greasy burger and wash it down with the first of many more beers that day and night."

"I don't think Bourbon is ever truly clean except for early Ash Wednesday morning after the cleaning machines come out to mop up all the crap," Tim laughed.

The two men continued to the east, often nearly losing their balance from stepping on the beads, which rolled beneath their feet like in an old cartoon. The neon of the signs affront the bars and daiquiri shops had been shut off for now. Lavish and expensive hotels gave reprieve from the endless parade of watering holes, as did authentic Creole and seafood restaurants with their aromas adrift into the street to battle the stench of stale alcohol. Soon, the clubs and strip joints faded and were replaced with lofty rainbow flags that flew above the gay bars.

"Hey, Jimbo," Tim burst as he nudged James's arm. "Remember the time we—"

"Yeah, I remember," he cut his friend off with no desire to relive the experience.

Tim's smile faded as he eyed James for a moment, and then brought his gaze back forward. James found himself brooding, wounded and hurt. At times, what Tim had done to him years before slipped James's mind, especially when they had fun. But at other times, there grew a sour mood. He turned sullen and bitter. His answers grew short as he looked at Tim with disgust. It was understandable. It was a time to rebuild trust.

As the two turned to the southeast toward the river, beer havens became high-end shops and hotels. Ahead, some blocks away, the old Ursuline Convent gleamed in the March sunshine. The Roman Catholic Church took care of its buildings. Its light gray stucco was in nearly perfect condition. It appeared as if it could have been built a decade ago, despite being over two hundred and fifty years old.

Finally, James and Tim turned the corner to see the Beauregard home a block away. They both became somewhat conscious of the previous night's events, and slowed their approach in caution. They looked for any sign that there had been an intruder, yet the only thing they saw out of the ordinary was their new friend Dr. Rylan Reed waiting for them at the lower level of the house below the columned porch. Somehow, that gave them comfort, and they sped their step.

"Hello, Dr. Reed." James extended his hand for a shake, as did Tim. "Crazy night, huh?"

"I would agree," he said with a grin. "That's more excitement than I've seen in quite some time. Makes me feel young again."

"You didn't happen to see any sign of a break-in or anything did you?" James spoke slowly as he peered up at the porch and the yellow stucco façade.

"I've been here for about twenty minutes, and I haven't seen a thing," he replied with a motion to the front door.

"Okay," James sighed, and led the way up one of the dual staircases. "We've got to get our stuff, and then we can be off. I see you already have your suitcase, Dr. Reed."

James ascended the left staircase to his front porch, and inserted his key into the deadbolt. He turned the key to find that the bolt did not move—only the tumbler. It was already unlocked. He watched Tim's face turn white. James's face held more anger than fear. He turned his attention back to the door and rotated the knob slowly to crack it and peer inside. As he did not see any danger, the gap between the door and the frame widened until there was enough room to move inside.

"I don't see anything out of the ordinary," James said with apprehension as he looked around at the kitchen foyer area.

"Maybe Noelle accidentally left it unlocked," Tim suggested as the other two men fanned out across the house. "I'm sure she left last night in a panic."

"Scratch that," Reed said from the office area.

Tim and James quickly scurried over to see that the drawers in his desk were left open and papers scattered across the crimson floorboards. Most of the books, including the rare ones, were tossed from the shelves. The fine Persian rugs were ruffled and the furniture was moved out of the normal places. James bolted from the office and around the corner to check the status of the bedrooms down the hall. In each he looked into, the bed sheets were piled onto the floor and the mattresses were off-center on the box springs. Closets gaped open with belongings strewn from inside to out. James reached his late son's room. He hadn't touched it in years. It was preserved like a museum. But to see it now caused red in his face the color of his boiling blood.

"This wasn't a burglary, James," Tim yelled across the house from the office. "All the electronics are still here," he said as James walked into the office, still fuming. "All the antiques and rare books are still here. Hell, if this was a gang-banger hit, the door would have been kicked in. They don't pick locks."

"I agree," Reed said, and nodded with concern. "They were looking for something in particular."

"Like these?" James carefully removed the Lafitte journal pages from his jacket pocket.

Each of them stood there for a few moments in silence. They pivoted on their heels in disbelief, and examined the tossed office with a feeling of full violation. It hurt. It was so much more personal than a simple mugging.

"All right," James uttered, and pulled it together. "I'm going to go pack a bag. Tim, grab your shit and we'll be out the door in a few minutes."

"We're still going?" Tim asked in disbelief, the situation now far too real. "You think we should really be getting involved with this?"

"What am I supposed to do?" James motioned to the trashed room. "Am I supposed to just wait around until Connor or whoever the hell this was comes back and points a gun in my face? At Noelle? Screw that," he continued as he watched Tim hang his head. "Besides, what if there's something to all this? What if there is some sort of power that needs to be kept from the wrong hands? There's some group of people out there that have spent the last two hundred years looking for this figurine and these pages. They obviously mean business. So we're going to go to Galveston and hope they don't clue into that being the next step."

Chapter 6

Cool air rushed in from the dark London streets, and coursed within the warmth of the old pub. People inside enjoyed spirits and conversations quietly along the bar and at the fine hardwood tables. They shuddered a bit, and even turned to get a brief glimpse at the person who unsettled them. A casually-dressed man, in jeans and a black leather jacket, did not keep the door open long. He allowed it to shut and moved his short, rotund figure across the pub where he spotted his friend.

The pub was very dim, which provided an almost somber mood. Patrons paid no more attention to this new arrival. The warmth and ale had each in a bubble that excluded any outside stimulus. The stubby newcomer moved past and amongst them. He rubbed his receding and thinning hair nervously as he crossed the room. He continued past the long, brightly-lit bar. A tall, thin middle-aged barkeep, clad in his usual white apron, nodded as he cleaned a beer mug with a rag. The old wooden walls were adorned with cricket and soccer paraphernalia from jerseys to outdated old equipment. It was a favorite neighborhood place with a lot of history and a lot of soul.

He reached a darker back corner of the pub and stepped up to the final booth. He stopped, crouched with a grunt, and plopped his large rear end onto the red leather cushioning. As he struggled to slide down and settle in, a much more physically fit gentleman of perhaps the same age leaned forward to rest his elbows on the solid tabletop. With a pleasant demeanor, he drank his red ale with delight then licked any residue from his stubbly upper lip.

"Get you something to drink, sir?" A waitress appeared, almost out of thin air.

"Oh, yes," the heavier man said, startled. "Newcastle," he ordered politely.

"I'll have one, too," the man across the table added.

They simply stared at one another for several moments. The low droning of pub sounds surrounded them like a cloud as they patiently awaited the delivery of their beer. And as if they willed it to happen at that moment, the waitress appeared with the two pints, and slid them into position for consumption.

"I've received word," the heavier man leaned in and spoke quietly.

"Yes? From New Orleans?"

"One of our operatives on permanent location there confirmed it," he replied. "Someone has located the lost journal entries inside Lafitte's Blacksmith Shop."

"Of course. We always knew it was there. Who found it?"

"An academic," he shrugged. "A Dr. James Beauregard and a friend of his. We've done some digging on Beauregard, and we're still working on the identity of his friend."

"How did they figure out the pages were there?"

"Apparently a chance discovery beneath Andrew Jackson's statue," the heavy man said. "A letter from Lafitte to his son. Something in it pointed them to the blacksmith shop. It doesn't matter. What matters is they've found it."

"And our operative is tailing them? Reporting back?"

"Well, he made a little mistake. He tried to take the pages from them right outside the blacksmith shop. He failed, and they've disappeared."

"Shit, and now he's burned his cover," he growled, and pounded his fist on the table. "They've disappeared?"

"They didn't return to their house, and we've searched it without finding anything except some light research on the blacksmith shop and someone named Pierre Lafleur on their internet browser history," he replied. "But they're nowhere to be found. We're still waiting on confirmation as to where they are or where they're heading. Last I've heard from the Chancellor, he wants more personnel sent to the United States to pursue this."

"Okay." The thinner man nodded solemnly. "It's a start—we're closer than we've been in two hundred years. I'll relay this to the others in the Society and we'll discuss the plan of action. Hopefully we can get in touch with the Chancellor. I can't believe it. Finally, it will be ours again. I'm going to try to call my father. I want to go to the U.S. myself."

Chapter 7

Dr. Rylan Reed had a disgusted sort of expression on his face as he emerged from the passageway in the back. He was an aging vision of European class in an unruly rural Louisiana setting. A faint noise of the outdated toilet churned in the back of the hallway behind him. He only took a single step every few moments, distracted by the mobile phone in his hand, and then he shoved it into the pocket of his beige wool blazer. Around him was the world of American consumerism. He turned his head in every direction, allowing himself to be permeated by it all.

The dingy, off-white sheetrock walls were stained and smeared by years of dirty hands and lack of cleaning. An entire wall was devoted to cooler space with a seemingly endless row of glass doors, behind which dozens of drinks of every variety faded to the right. There was branding everywhere, from the stacks of twelve-packs of soda cans that lined the walls to the endless array of chips, candy, and junk food that adorned the rows of shelves in the center of the store. Even the walls and windows were decorated with neon beer signs and wall-height banners of scantily-clad models who were set on the seduction of men into purchasing their brand of brew.

Reed continued on to the counter area, which was directly parallel to the double glass doors to the left. It was a gorgeous day, the nearly cloudless sky a deep royal blue in the midday sun. The light poured through the windows to drown the crude, artificial fluorescent bulbs that hummed in the rectangular glass spaces in the ceiling.

There, James stood between the lottery scratch-offs and a small case full of very cheap, truck driver-grade souvenirs like Zippos decorated with Confederate flags and low quality folding knives with skulls and wolves on them. He stood, wallet in hand, awaiting the badly aged woman to finish bagging and give him the total.

"That'll be thirteen fifty-seven, hun." The woman finally looked tiredly up at James, the bags under her eyes puffy and defined.

"All right." James took a twenty from his wallet, and handed it to the woman.

She tossed her curly, late Eighties hair style from her shoulders with a whip of her head. Her expression never changed from a bit of a permanent scowl as she looked at the bill. She eyed it closely as she pressed a few buttons on the dated register to send the drawer to open with a bang.

"Here you are, baby." She finally handed James his change and slid the brown paper bag across the counter like a Fifties soda jerk.

"Thank you, ma'am," James said as he pocketed the change. "Have a great day." He turned for the door as she forced a smile that seemed like more of a wince.

He caught sight of Reed as he turned and moved for the door, almost startled in the revelation that he was standing there. They approached the double doors, pressed the metal release bar with a clang, and exited the gas station into the humid South Louisiana air mingled with gasoline fumes and traces of exhaust. The day grew warmer, almost too warm for Reed's blazer and James's thin hoodie. They squinted in defense against the ultra-bright rays as James pulled his sunglasses from where they rested atop his head, and placed them across the bridge of his nose.

"I think she was a bit sweet on you," Reed said as they both walked toward the Tahoe.

James had no response except for a little grin of acknowledgement and slight amusement. They continued to stroll across the oil-stained concrete toward the Tahoe at one of the far pumps. Tim had just finished filling the tank and removed the nozzle from the opening.

"How much was it?" James asked as he strode up to Tim.

"Eighty bucks," he responded, and jerked the receipt from the pump's printer.

"Jesus!" James remarked, almost angry. "I should have never bought this gas-guzzler."

"Hey, don't complain," Tim responded as he opened the back door to crawl inside. "You ought to see how much gas has been up north."

"Or in England." Reed opened the front passenger door, stepped up onto the running board, and slid onto the black leather seat. "This price you pay per gallon of petrol is nothing compared to Europe."

"I guess I can't complain," James said as he stepped up into the driver's seat and started the engine. "But I will anyway." He pulled at the lever and clicked into gear.

The Tahoe rolled across the concrete and past the last gas pump until it stopped where the driveway met the darker asphalt of the street. James could see the bustling interstate to his left as he looked for the ramp and the signs. Slowly, he turned the wheel to the left and rolled onto the street parallel to the bayou that ran beneath the interstate bridge. The bayou was lined on both sides with thick, well-kept centipede grass embankments. A giant, centuries-old live oak twisted its gnarly trunk toward the sky, where its branches hung with thick, curly Spanish moss. It was the wise old woman of the swamp. Its big roots below curled and lumped from out of the soil and back in as if it were a nest of anacondas within the ground.

James drove the vehicle up to the stop sign and looked from left to right before he continued on, banking right onto the ramp that led up to the interstate. He accelerated to nearly the speed limit of the highway and signaled before he merged.

"Easy, killer," Tim said from the back seat. "You just burned up a quarter of a tank getting onto the interstate."

"God, I hate this drive." James dug a beef jerky out of his brown bag full of junk food. "Anyone?" he asked as he held up the bag to offer the salty meat to his friends.

"No thank you." Reed sneered a bit.

"How can you eat this shit and stay in shape?" Tim scowled.

"I don't eat junk food regularly," he said. "It's a *sometimes* food. I walk to most places in the Quarter, I jog a few times a week, and we usually cook pretty healthy organic food."

"But you go on a road trip and fall off the wagon?"

"A bag of beef jerky two or three times a year isn't going to make me fat or give me a heart attack," James defended. "It's not my breakfast every morning. It's pure protein. It's better than chips or candy full of carbs and sugar."

"Why do you hate this drive?" Reed asked. "It's beautiful. That long bridge earlier with all the swamp and cypress trees—that was gorgeous."

"The Atchafalaya basin," Tim provided the name.

"Yes," Reed continued. "You don't see things like that in Europe. I can't believe I've never seen all this. I've always focused so much on New Orleans that I've never bothered with seeing the bayous of the Cajun region."

"You ought to come back out this way during Mardi Gras," Tim suggested. "New Orleans is great, but if you want to get down to roots, go see the Mamou parade. The floats are all horse-drawn and rustic. People run around chasing chickens and shit. It's more family-friendly, the Cajuns are always down-to-earth, and holy crap, they can cook!"

"Sounds amazing." Reed glanced back at Tim, and then redirected his attention to James, awaiting an answer.

"I know, the scenery here is pretty," James shrugged. "I guess I'm just used to it. But all this swamp—the flora and fauna—ends in a few miles. It turns to walls of woods on either side of the interstate, and then it just becomes an endless parade of oil refineries and industrial areas. And it's long—a long drive," he explained.

"It does get better once you get into Texas, though," Tim commented from the backseat. "Once you get over into Beaumont, you're home free until Galveston."

"True," James confirmed.

Conversation stopped for miles. There was something about the hum of rubber on the road in combination with the seamless stream of white and yellow lines that passed the vehicle. It lulled the three travelers into a stupor. The hypnotized professors had lost all power to their mouths, unable to speak, though they may have wanted to. James found some comfort in watching the road and passing drivers who travelled slower. He constantly searched for satellite radio stations with the controls built into his steering wheel. He surfed through a parade of Nineties and alternative rock stations, mingled with the occasional country or comedy channel. Reed just stared blankly through the windshield, and then through the side window when he got bored with that.

Tim said nothing, which was a rare occasion. But the boredom set in, and he was frustrated with the music James selected. His saving grace was his smartphone. He surfed, searched, and used his social networking applications to keep him occupied, and since he had packed a car charger, he had no fear of the battery being drained.

"Holy shit," he exclaimed, breaking the silence within the cab of the SUV.

"What?" James jumped and then peered at Tim through the rearview mirror.

"I was searching Nicholas Lockyer, and I found something interesting." Tim stared at his phone. "You said," he motioned to Reed, "that Captain Nicholas Lockyer was one of the guys who propositioned Jean Lafitte to help the British attack the Americans at New Orleans, right?"

"That's correct." Reed squinted attentively and turned in his seat.

"Well, I ended up on some conspiracy theory website where he was listed as a member and even head of a secret society that existed in England."

"What's the society called?" James inquired as he briefly looked up into the rearview mirror.

"The Society of the Lost Dominion," Tim read from his phone.

"I've heard of this one," Reed popped. "As I recall, it was begun in the seventeen eighties—just after the American Revolution."

"That's right," Tim confirmed, and continued to read from his phone. "This says that King George III was extremely distraught over losing the American colonies."

"To the point that he went mad," James interrupted. "Like, certifiable."

"Yeah. This site says George founded a secret society that included nobles, high-born military leaders, and even businessmen that lost a lot of profit from the loss of the colonies."

"To what end?" James scoffed a bit. "Was it like the modern KKK? Did they just sit around, bitching and moaning about who they hate—complain about how much it sucked to lose the North American colonies?"

"According to this site, it was a bit more than just bitching about losing the colonies," Tim said. "Apparently, they're suspected to have been active. When British sailors in the Atlantic started raiding American ships and conscripting their sailors, that was the society's doing."

"And hence the U.S. declaration of war on Britain," Reed said in acceptance of the theory. "They lost out on a lot of raw materials from North American—particularly the timber that built the ships for His Majesty's Navy. It was an opportunity to regain the colonies—a rematch of the Revolution, if you will."

"So it seems natural that they would send some of their military members to the mouth of the Mississippi, and see what they could do to capture the country's most important port," James agreed.

"And there's where Lockyer and Lafitte come in," Tim said. "It doesn't actually say this on the website. Maybe no one's made the connection—it's too obscure for most people's general historical knowledge. The site states that members of the Society included General George Prevost, Lieutenant General Drummond, Rear Admiral George Cockburn, Captain Nicholas Lockyer, and even Lieutenant Edward Packenham—who led the charge at the Battle of New Orleans."

"A hero at Waterloo, struck down in the Louisiana Swamps," Reed said bitterly, as the other two men looked at him strangely and then shrugged it off.

"Makes sense, doesn't it?" Tim continued his argument. "All these military leaders part of a major push to regain the 'lost dominion'?"

"Even the name references the Imperial British term *dominion*," James thought out loud. "It's a mostly self-governing British colony. The lost dominion in question certainly could refer to the U.S."

"And so Lockyer, a member of the Society, could easily have been sent as an operative to recruit Lafitte and the Barataria privateers," Tim concluded.

"But it didn't work, and the war was lost, along with New Orleans," James said. "Does it say anything about the Society continuing to send guys to New Orleans after eighteen fifteen?"

"No." Tim looked again at his phone, and then back toward the men in the front seats. "There's no information after the War of 1812. It's as if the Society just disappeared. And that makes sense. There were no more wars with Britain—eventually alliances are made."

"Yeah, but not until the twentieth century," James argued. "And even then, a secret society can continue their idealistic quest separately from the pro-U.S. government."

"Lafitte said in his letter that he did not want the jaguar to fall into the wrong hands," Tim said. "The Battle of New Orleans occurred a few weeks after the war was officially over."

"Yeah," James said, "no modern communication. They had no idea the war was over."

"What if they did know?" Tim suggested. "And what if the Battle of New Orleans didn't have a thing to do with the capture of the Mississippi River? What if it had everything to do with the capture of this jaguar figurine? Lafitte said in his journal that Englishmen tried to kill him several times. What if they were members of this Society—operatives still trying to get the jaguar?"

"Causing him to hide the journal entries, and haul ass out of Louisiana." James's eyes lit up. "And then he heads to Galveston. And even then, he eventually has to leave Galveston for South America."

"Or Mayan country?" Reed suggested. "Guatemala is where he went next—the center of the Mayan world."

"Shit, this is huge!" James gasped. "Do you think these guys are still in operation? Surely Dr. Conner was one of them if that's the case. A secret society sleeper cell at Tulane!"

"They had to have been in eighteen fifty-three, when Lafleur, or

Lafitte, hid the letter under Jackson's statue," Tim said. "So why not now?"

"There's something to this jaguar thing." James sounded convinced. He thought for a moment. "And we have to find it."

Chapter 8

With a light jolt of reaching the dock, the Galveston ferry had reached its destination, along with dozens of personal vehicles from the Bolivar Peninsula to the island. James's silver Tahoe had been parked on the deck for half an hour already, sandwiched between a small red sport coupe and a giant pickup that was jacked up and perched upon massive mud tires. *Small penis*, James thought to himself as he looked at the truck through his rearview mirror. He wondered how much longer it was going to take. He enjoyed the company of his two friends for the most part, but being in such a confined space with anyone for too long can make a person itch to be free.

Tightness built in his muscles. He had tried to ignore it, but that just was not in James's character. On the road, he had control of the wheel and the accelerator. Even in the unfortunate event of a near accident, he had control to be able to avoid a collision. He enjoyed being the master of his destiny. Being in his car on the ferry was akin to a straitjacket. His fingers drummed on the wheel as he bobbed in his seat. His lips puckered and molars clenched together as the beginnings of a headache lingered somewhere behind his eyeballs.

It did not, however, take very long to prepare for the unloading of the ferry. This ferry ran practically non-stop for most of the day, every day. The process was down to a fine science, and as soon as the ferry was properly moored and secured, engines cranked and came to life as cars and trucks filed from in front of him. In little time, James was able to apply pressure to the accelerator and pull off the ferry and onto the concrete lanes of Ferry Road.

Gulls swirled overhead as the sun drooped in the west. The coast bore a different kind of energy. The cracked boulevard held few indications of being near a beach just yet. Small, ramshackle houses in a neighborhood to the right of Ferry Road were poorly kept, most with paint chipping from the wood siding that topped the concrete blocks which kept the structures elevated in times of storm surge. But a neighborhood like that could easily exist in any city. Aside from the seagulls and flatness of the terrain, one could wake up in this place and have no clue they were near the beach. But still, there was a different energy that came with being near the water.

Soon it was more obvious that they were in vacation territory. The boulevard curved to the right, and with the approaching sight of the beach ahead, the small shacks that lined Ferry Road were but a memory that was overshadowed by more picturesque local residences. Victorian cottages and two-story nineteen thirties bungalows formed more affluent neighborhoods accented with palm trees and other tropical vegetation. The beachfront street was lined with giant corporate hotels, spas, and resorts. Beach shops of only a few variations were on every corner and provided souvenirs, swimsuits, towels, and sunscreen to vacation-goers. It possessed a single drop of essence similar to Key West, and perhaps that is what Galveston attempted to accomplish. But still, this was coastal Texas—not the Florida Keys. No amount of resorts and beach shops could mask the brownish, mud-filled water.

"It finally feels like a vacation." Tim excitedly leaned toward his window and peered with a smile at bikini-clad coeds who walked the streets and beaches in the unusually warm weather. "I'm so glad we're at the beach. What do you say, guys? Hit some clubs tonight, and worry about all this Lafitte shit in the morning?"

"I hate Galveston," James said, expressionless.

"Why? It's the beach."

"It's *a* beach," James fired back. "But it's not vacation-worthy. I'd rather go somewhere like the Florida panhandle. That's a nearby paradise. Why couldn't Lafitte have hidden the jaguar thing near Destin? At least the water there is clear and blue. It's not this dirty, dingy, shitty water they have here. We may as well be in Biloxi or something."

"At least Biloxi has casinos," Tim commented.

"Well I, for one, think this place is lovely," Reed said as he peered out the window. "I've never been here. Seeing a new place is always exciting. Besides, this is a better beach than I can find at home in the UK."

That's an understatement, James mused. "Which hotel did you book?" He spoke to Tim through the rearview mirror.

"The only place I could get a room was at the Seaview Resort," Tim said as he held up his smartphone. "It's four hundred bucks a night, so I expect you to pay me back your share."

"Jesus." James's jaw dropped.

"Spring break, dude," Tim shrugged. "We're in a resort town during spring break. They're gonna jack up the prices. This place is full of Aggies and Longhorns ready to get drunk and laid, all on daddy's credit card."

"This had to happen during spring break," James scowled. "Two hotel rooms in two days, and both in prime locations during peak season."

The SUV continued along the beachfront road as resorts and surf shops passed along the way. Tim drooled over young breasts covered with thin layers of material as James searched for the hotel. Finally, partially hidden by the glare of the setting sun, he spotted the small, motel-looking hotel. He could have easily missed it with such a small sign. As he slowed and turned into the driveway, he was amazed at what little four hundred dollars bought him. Ugly, urbanesque parking lots completely surrounded the front and sides of the four-story hotel. There was little to dress it up, only a small patch of grass in front, a few shrubs, and flagpoles waving the banners of the U.S., Texas, and the red Seaview logo.

The Tahoe pulled in under the awning affront the automatic doors that led into the lobby, and James shifted into park and pulled the keys from the ignition. The three professors opened their doors and stepped down from the elevated cab. They bent, contorted, and stretched their muscles in almost an unnatural fashion. Their faces made ugly, grimaced expressions and their joints popped to release tension that came with sitting in the same position for hours.

James popped open the hatch of the vehicle, and the men pulled their suitcases from the back. The wheels of the suitcases groaned and popped rhythmically with every seam they hit between bricks. The automatic doors slid open and allowed a sudden and almost unwelcome burst of cold air conditioning to rush over their bodies.

The lobby was not extravagant. Plain beige tiles covered every inch of the interior's floor. There was a small seating area to the right with a few couches and chairs positioned around a wall-mounted television that was set to some news channel. Just beyond lay a small dining area with perhaps a dozen and a half small tables with cheap-looking chairs. A single, slightly outdated computer sat at a tiny desk in the far corner of the lobby. No one used it. College kids teemed within the space either heading to or from the elevators down the hall, most of them in swimsuits or comfortable shorts and tees. They all appeared somewhat intoxicated already, and perhaps a bit pink.

The three men banked left, their suitcases in tow, and found the long, plain wooden counter of the front desk. Behind it, a tall, fat man with long braided chin hair filled his triple-extra large Hawaiian shirt to its maximum capacity. He wore a Rasta knit beanie over his shaggy, greasy hair, which complemented his bloodshot eyes.

"What can I do for you guys?" His deep voice was slow and labored.

"Yeah, we have a reservation under Horn Chamberlain," Tim said as he stepped up to the chest-high countertop.

"Not only did you register under an alias like you're a rock star," James laughed, "but you used your porn-star name."

"Hey, don't knock it. We've got a crazy-ass secret society after us. An alias might come in handy."

They both stopped their conversation, and looked toward the large man who assisted them. He stood swaying a bit from side to side, as his hairy arms hung almost lifelessly. His expression was blank and clueless as he stared at James and Tim, and then he finished processing. He then gave only one response—a lazy grin followed by a burned out chuckle.

"Yeah," the man searched through the computer. "We have your reservation. I'll just use the card number on file in case of incidental charges and movie orders," he continued, and then typed and clicked a few times with the mouse to confirm the check-in. "Here are your keys." He slid two card keys across the worn wooden counter. "Room three seventeen. Here's your parking hanger. You have to put that on your mirror in your car if you don't want to be towed. You can park anywhere in the parking lot. Is there anything else I can help you with?"

"Nope." Tim grabbed the keys and handed one of them to James, as well as the parking tag. "Thanks a lot."

"See you guys in the room. Take my suitcase for me, will you?" James then turned and headed for the front door as the others made their way down the hall to the elevators.

After parking the SUV in the lot, James stepped again into the lobby and walked across the damp, gritty tile floors to the elevator lobby. He pressed the "UP" button on the wall, illuminating it in a Kool-Aid red glow, and waited for a short time before the center elevator chimed and opened. From the all-steel walls stepped three young men and two flirty young women, all loud and rowdy. James could smell the aroma of cheap whiskey from the extra large plastic cups in their hands. That was an all too familiar smell. It brought to his mind sweet thoughts that danced with darkness and tragedy. He shook off the emotion and stepped inside the industrial steel confines of the elevator.

He could not wait to get out of the elevator. Though he was alone inside, it was cramped. That is the way it seemed, at least. He disliked small enclosed spaces without windows. It felt unnatural. He could never tell exactly what was happening or what was to happen. He simply tried to breathe deeply the alcoholic air and calm himself for a short time until the doors would open and allow him to break free.

He finally reached the third floor, and stepped gladly into the hallway. The walls were classic taupe, lined with endless doors and placards displaying the room numbers beneath shiny Plexiglas. The carpets were thick, gaudy red-and-gold-paisley decorating nightmares.

He traversed the length of the hallway, scanning the numbers to the side of each door until he found room three seventeen. He dug into his back pocket, and pulled the thin, credit card-like piece of plastic out, and accessed the door.

"Where's Tim?" he asked Reed as he looked around the room.

"He's in the bathroom about to take a shower," Reed responded. "We met some girls in the hallway and they're partying in their room down the hall. I don't think they're old enough to drink in the bars. Either way, they invited us to join them."

"So Tim is going to take advantage of some poor drunk college freshman? Classic. And you?"

"I'm going, too." Reed grinned. "Why not?"

"Come with us, Jimbo!" Tim's voice echoed from the bathroom. "No one will ever know."

"Nope. You guys have fun. I'm going to call Noelle and let her know we made it."

"Pussy," Tim responded.

Chapter 9

The man from the London pub ambled through the crowds, trailed closely by a cohort. Nick was tall and handsome, his spiked, dirty-blond hair meticulously tossed with putty to achieve the look of being disheveled. He strode with a confident swagger that came naturally, a stark contrast against that of his cohort.

The space within which he walked was sensory overload. The hum and metallic sounds of the stainless steel conveyors blended with the constant drone of hundreds of conversations that take place all at once. Throngs of people with satchels and backpacks thrown over their shoulders huddled around the conveyors, as they poked their heads above the backs of others in an attempt to see if their luggage had finally moved along the steel belts. They pushed and prodded into every inch of space around the conveyors, frustrated and travel weary. Television screens hung in their lofty positions above the crowds with flight statuses for arrivals, departures, delays, and cancellations. People recklessly strode across the nearly industrial tile floors with roller suitcases behind them.

Nick remained calm, unaffected by the mayhem. He never lost his cool or allowed himself to lose his temper. He just let anything adverse roll off him like a water-proofed raincoat in a spring shower. It simply beaded up and rolled away, leaving not even a trail behind it.

He moved in the direction of the exit and the diminished evening sun that painted everything outside a deep, rosy color. He kept his eyes forward, readjusted the small duffel bag on his shoulder, and reached into the pockets of his faded jeans to dig for his mobile phone. It took him a few moments, unable to gain just the perfect grip. Finally, he was able to take it between his thumb and index finger, and then pull the black rectangular device from his pocket. He lifted it before his face and scrolled through his contacts list on the glass touch screen to make his call.

"We're here," his deep, London accent registered in the speaker. "Just got off the plane."

The voice on the other end was audible to anyone passing by, yet indiscernible in what was being said. Nick listened attentively as he walked.

"Yes," he responded. "We'll get some rest tonight and head to Galveston bright and early." He stopped and waited for speaking on the other end, visibly annoyed with what he heard. "Yes, I'm sure," he spoke. "We'll leave as early as we can and beat the traffic. We'll be on time—I promise. Okay. Okay. Goodbye." He pressed the screen to end the call, and put it back into his pocket with a roll of his eyes.

"The old man giving you hell?" the short, pudgy cohort smirked as he sped his stride to catch up.

"As always," Nick expressed, annoyed. "Look, no escapades with loose American women tonight. We have to be in Galveston early," he half mocked at the man to his side.

"You've got it."

Chapter 10

"Slummin' it," James said as he drove the silver SUV into the drive-through lane and up to the ordering intercom box of the coffee shop.

It was a very nice coffee shop, at least. It was not fronted by cheap, painted concrete, nor did it have weeds growing from cracks in the driveway. It was constructed with fine red brick, and one could see through the windows that it had nice terra cotta tile and deep, rusty brown-colored walls in the interior. The front and sides of the building featured nicely-manicured hedges and freshly planted flowers of all colors, which bloomed in the mild air. But none of this mattered as much to James. It could be a rotten wooden shack worthy of condemnation for all he cared.

"What? Why?" Tim raised his eyebrows.

"We're resorting to the bottom-of-the-barrel, average corporate coffee shop," James sneered. "This stuff sucks. We're better off with the crap they put in the hotel room next to the little coffee maker." No one commented.

"Can I take your order?" a droll female voice buzzed from the speaker with a level of distortion that was enough to make one's skin crawl.

"Um, yeah." James then turned to his passengers, suddenly panicked that he had not asked them what they wanted. His eyes shifted frantically between Tim and Reed, sure that the girl on the inside grew impatient by the second.

"Just a coffee—black," Reed said.

"Like your coffee like you like your women?" James snickered with the tired old joke.

"Yes," Reed paused. "Chopped up, and in the freezer."

"Non-fat mocha latte," Tim belted, caught off-guard by Reed's response.

"Okay." James turned back to the intercom with a smirk. "Two large coffees—one black and one with two creams and three sugars."

"Will that be all?" the girl cut him off.

"No, I wasn't done." He rolled his eyes. "The last thing is a non-fat mocha latte."

"Nine fifty-two," she sighed as the distortion almost rendered her words incomprehensible. "Pull up to the window, please."

"When did you become such a woman?" James poked at his friend as he eased the Tahoe to the window.

"Whatever," Tim shot back. "I drink what I like, so shut it."

"Americans have the strangest way of expressing their friendship," Reed half said to himself.

The small drive-through window slid open and popped as it crashed to a halt against the stopper. On the other side stood a petite young high school girl with long black hair. She was well-dressed with the finest makeup from the most expensive of department stores. But her expression was of loathing. She appeared to not have had much sleep, and moved about with sluggishness and discontent.

"Nine fifty-two." She rolled her eyes and extended her hand. James handed her a debit card, which she quickly swiped and handed right back to him. "You know; you didn't have to be so rude."

"Rude?" He narrowed his brow. "Me? You're the one who cut me off in the middle of my order like you couldn't wait to get me out of your hair so you could go on screwing with your phone, and counting the minutes until it's time to go home. How old are you? Seventeen? Eighteen? I bet you can't wait to move out of your parents' house so you can do whatever you want, but then expect them to pay your way as they always have. Let me guess. Daddy wanted to teach you some work ethic so he made you get a job to pay your own car insurance, your cell phone bill, or buy your own clothes. But the damage is already done, isn't it, darling? You've never had to earn a thing in your life, and it just kills you to have to go out, be responsible, and be held accountable for something, just like the rest of your generation."

She simply stood there for a moment, her mouth wide in shock and even hurt. She physically reeled, appalled at what was said to her. Tim and Reed looked away. If they could have distanced themselves, they would have.

"That is so not true," the girl finally responded in a snappy sort of voice.

"And there's the other thing," James railed again. "You've been living in cyber-world for so long that you can't handle face-to-face confrontation to save your life."

"God, you sound like my teachers," she said as she reluctantly handed over the three coffees in a brown paper drink holder.

"I *am* a teacher, sweetie." He smiled and took the coffee. "We all sound like this, and that should tell you something. Have a nice day." He handed the drink holder to Tim, and sped out of the drive-through, quite satisfied.

The Tahoe pulled out into the street and made a left toward the north away from the gulf. Downtown Galveston was a nice little town, rich with diversity in history, culture, and architecture. It was as if a Texas cow town had stopped in to pick up New Orleans, and moved to Key West. The buildings ranged from giant three-story granite former department stores on the corners to flat-fronted two-story Victorian shops along the streets. The deep brown brick and faded old advertisements and signs on the sides of the buildings were accented by palm trees and the sound of seagulls in the near distance.

Tourists strolled the concrete sidewalks and frequented shops of every sort in the same way that they did in New Orleans. And they visited similar places. There were seafood restaurants next to Texas barbecue joints. Souvenir shops sold everything from Galveston t-shirts to waterproof disposable cameras, swimsuits, and beach towels. People took full advantage of the warming air. Short sleeves and shorts accompanied sunglasses across every nose. Young women on spring vacation ambled along in bikini tops and short-shorts and made every effort to seem appealing to male passersby.

"I see you're reaching out to the young people," Tim commented to his friend. "I don't think that little girl in the drive-through was quite prepared for that."

"I don't get these kids," he replied. "People used to be so worried about their self-esteem, and now they have too much of it. They have self-esteem for no good reason. It's to the point they don't feel the need to earn it anymore."

"It's a different generation," Tim shrugged. "Not worse. Just different. Our parents thought we were retarded, too. They didn't understand us. And we turned out okay. We're contributing members of society. And society just evolves. It does no good to berate these kids. You have to connect to them."

"What about you? Did you *connect* with any college girls last night?" he asked with the stink of sarcasm. "You woke up next to *me*. I half expected you to roll in this morning, tired and reeking of sex and whiskey."

"I think we were more likely regarded as the creepy old geezers that try to hang out with the young people," Reed chimed in. "I ended up sitting there sipping a cheap can of beer by myself. So I just came back to the room early."

"Couldn't seal the deal, Tim?"

"I guess I'm just getting old." He shook his head in defeat. "I see them every day in the classroom, and even at Yale, I don't understand their lingo, their obsession with their phones, and certainly their music. I'd much rather be listening to Pearl Jam, and most of these kids think it's something that goes on toast. I do my best in an academic sense. But as far as last night goes . . . well . . . maybe I should switch to cougar hunting. Am I out of touch?"

"I wouldn't say out of touch," James sympathized. "It's just part of getting older. You long for the way things used to be because those were the best times of your life. And then the gap appears between you and the younger generation. Accept it, dude. Be the older, wiser voice of reason to them. Generativity. And I wouldn't worry about getting their music. Their music sucks. Our music is timeless. It remains relevant. Pop represents youth—songs about dating, clubbing, and breakups. It comes and goes. That's not us anymore. It's all aching knees and hemorrhoid cream."

The island was long, but not wide. It did not take long to reach the bay side of the island. The Tahoe approached from the south, still a few blocks away from Harborside Drive. The scenery ahead became much less pleasing to the eye than the lively downtown areas behind them. The seaport's sandy-colored façade and dingy concrete gave the look of industry rather than tourism. There were no cruise ships towering behind to give it that feel. It just appeared as a long, seaside warehouse, enclosed by chain-link fences, and overshadowed by tall oil-drilling platforms behind, ready to be hauled out to sea.

"So where is this place?" Tim looked to the wharf ahead.

"Just like the port is on this side of the island now, it was in Lafitte's time, too." James continued to drive. "It's better protected from storms and gunboats ready to blast the place to holy hell."

"Not that it really protects from either of those things, really," Reed commented.

"Right," James agreed, and then continued. "Maison Rouge—the 'red house'—was Lafitte's private home, and it was likely the biggest structure on the island."

"Out of how many buildings, though?" Tim offered.

"More than you think. The colony numbered something like a thousand people at one time. This is where you came for plundered luxury items and newly-imported slaves. Even Jim Bowie did some smuggling out of here."

"But in eighteen seventeen, wouldn't the trade of imported slaves have been illegal in the U.S. by then?" Tim recalled.

"Yeah, but there was a loophole," James clarified. "You *could* sell slaves confiscated from foreign ships. That's why the *Amistad* case was such a big deal—it eliminated the loophole. But until then, that's what made this place highly lucrative."

"Not to mention the fact that this was not part of the United States in eighteen seventeen," Reed added. "It was part of Mexico."

"So did you find out where Maison Rouge was?" Tim asked again. "Wasn't it destroyed?"

"I did some research on this last night," James said as he turned right onto Harborside Drive. "The house survived Indian raids and was one of only six to survive a hurricane in eighteen eighteen. But in about eighteen twenty-one, the U.S. Navy came in and told Lafitte and his guys to get lost or they would be destroyed. So they hauled ass after burning everything."

"Which was when he took his family, dropped them in New Orleans, and went to Central America," Reed noted.

"Exactly. The house isn't there, but it's well-established that it was in a spot down here on Harborside Drive."

"Great." Tim rolled his eyes. "There's probably something built on the site. Real estate in this area is hot. There's no way we'll find what we're looking for. We can't just dig under someone's foundation while they're having breakfast."

"There *was* a house built on the site in eighteen seventy. Get this—it burned down not long after. The guy who lived there had gone crazy—something about strange dreams about being chased by a big jungle cat. The ruins of that are on top of the foundations of Maison Rouge. And since it's a registered Texas historical site, they won't let anyone build there."

"Apparently, a lot of treasure hunters have come in looking for buried booty and secret vaults," Reed said. "Rich businessmen come in with special sonar equipment and dig around. No one's ever found anything."

"Why would they think there's buried treasure on that spot?" James inquired through the rearview mirror.

"He had amassed a huge amount of loot, and when he left, it was just a few hours before the Navy's deadline," Reed answered. "They had lost ships in the hurricanes and such, so they didn't have the ability to take all of that with them. So it's speculated they buried it and left it behind. No one has ever found anything."

The cruise terminal faded to the rear and the port underwent a meta-morphosis into seaside markets and a few restaurants. Then even that gave way to less than congenial sights of shipyards, transportation equipment, and ugly chain-link fences, behind which was situated the public marina.

The glory and charm of downtown Galveston was gone now. The Victorian stores and shops shrunk in the mirrors, and they now entered quaint residential areas, industrial businesses, and even a University of Texas laboratory for the research of biomedics and exotic diseases. James looked carefully at the street signs at each intersection, and finally found the fourteen hundred block.

"Here we are." He pointed to the right as he tried to slow the vehicle.

Between a raised-foundation residence and a welding shop, they saw the unmistakable location they were looking for. It was a place that the modern world had forgotten. The concrete raised cellars that once supported a wooden home were now but a reminder of the once hab-itability of the location. On each side of the façade were two arched window compartments. In the center, concrete chipped from a core of red clay bricks to form a staircase to nothing above. Day after day, they deteriorated in the brutal Texas sun. Shrubs and grass threatened to lay siege to the lot and mosses and grass sprang from between the cracks in the central staircase.

"Jesus, that's it?" Tim locked his gaze upon the passing structure.

James signaled right and slowed the Tahoe before he turned down the residential street and parked alongside a small business of some sort that worked out of an old early twentieth century home. He wasted no time to park the SUV and exit. His colleagues followed, hesitant, but unquestioning of James's determination.

Sunglasses intact, they looked around for a moment to take in the sights and sounds. They cut down a little dirt driveway toward the site. Light powdery dust kicked into the gentle gulf breezes with each step. Their shoes became coated with a filthy gray layer of it as they trudged and no one uttered a word, as if afraid to do so.

"This looks like it." Tim approached the metal-fenced back end of the deep, narrow lot. They could each see the ruins further away, closer to the main street. "Here goes nothin'." He placed his hands between the rust-dusted top spikes of the chain-link fence, gained a firm grip on the top bar, and hoisted his fit body to the top, his shoes briefly perched before he hopped to the ground.

Dr. Reed watched with anxiety as Tim shrugged off the task as something nearly effortless. He then observed James smirk with his rare opportunity to display some youth in his advanced age. He followed the formula written in action by his friend to spring over the fence, and then they each looked over at their elder colleague.

"Come on, sir. We'll help you over." James motioned for Tim as they approached the fence with outstretched hands.

"Sir?" Reed frowned. "I'm not your grandfather," he protested, but allowed each man to grasp his middle-aged frame as he struggled to lift himself above.

He fought to place his feet into the fence squares and lift himself over. He threw a leg unsteadily over the top and caught his pants leg on one of the spikes. He shook and maneuvered amid grunts and panicked noises to free it, as finally his pants ripped down the side. He finally lifted his other leg over, and leaped to the ground, steadied by the hands of the amused men.

"You all right there, boss?" James grinned, and kept close to the professor to assure his steadiness.

"Oh, I think I'll survive." Reed hunched over to examine the tear in his fine trousers. "Damn. These were good pants."

"Can't wear classroom clothes to a treasure hunt," Tim mused as they all faced the lot they had entered.

Weeds had long polluted the grassy lot. It did not appear the city often cleared the high brush and nuisance shrubs. They multiplied like bacteria beneath the seat of a public toilet. The chaos of vegetation was maneuverable, so the men began to walk toward the remnants of the structural ruins.

"Do you Americans ever preserve anything?"

James stood at the old concrete perimeter and caressed the still-cool composite material. His fingertips read the bits of raised gravel as if it were telling him a story through Braille. Reed stepped through one of the arched openings in the old cellar, barely inside the confines. He stood and scanned his surroundings, almost afraid to go further in. Tim circled the perimeter to the front where a proud fortress structure once looked out over the bay, lording over the tides and every ship that rode them.

"Here it is," he yelled to the other two.

"Keep it down, jackass. We're trespassing, remember?" James whispered across the ruins. "What is it?"

"The Texas historical marker," he replied in a lower tone, now conscious of the prospect of possibly being arrested. "It says pretty much what you told us on the way here. Lafitte got here in about eighteen seventeen and left in about eighteen twenty-one, kicked out by the U.S. authorities, though they didn't control this island," he added the observation. "It says the buccaneers raided ships all over the gulf, and Lafitte furnished his house luxuriously from the booty. It also says there were holes cut into the upper floors for cannons."

"Cool." James worked his way around to the front beside Tim. "Brings new meaning to the idea of a home security system. I guess he needed the cannons high enough up to be able to carry the balls further out over the bay. He couldn't have done that through these holes in the cellar at ground level."

"This is the cellar?" Reed approached from within the remains of the structure, a perplexed look upon his face. "It's above the ground. Shouldn't a cellar be subterranean?"

"Not here," James replied. "It's not practical. The sand in the soil here isn't steady enough to support a large cellar. There would be no structural integrity."

"Not to mention flooding," Tim agreed. "Forget hurricanes—even just a strong gulf thunderstorm could flood an underground cellar right here, and it would take forever to clear it out," he added as Reed nodded in comprehension.

"My house is built the same way," James continued. "New Orleans is subject to flooding, so a lot of homes are raised and have cellars at ground level."

The three men stood silently beside the ruined old cellar remains as if the structure were some slumbering giant. One wrong move may wake it and send it into a fury. Something was gargantuan about it, though neither could tell from the structure itself. It was ominous, gloomy, and even creepy. But it held a secret. James could feel it.

"Do you think this is the cellar that was built for Maison Rouge, or is it from the later structure?" Tim pondered.

"That's a good question," James replied, and paused in thought. "I haven't read anything that said one way or another. But here's a better question. If Lafitte had cellars—and he did—he would have known to build it like this. If he hid the jaguar here and left it so no one would find it, where is it?" He motioned to the open-aired, above-ground cellar. "He wouldn't have left it here, above the ground. And if he did, then this thing is long gone."

"That's a good point." Reed scratched his head. "Surely he was smarter than that. He burned the place to the ground when he fled, and if he left the figurine behind intentionally, he would not have left it in an above-ground cellar."

James tuned out, his brain waves forming a cognitive barrier between him and any outside stimuli. He was lost in his own thought, oblivious to sound or even feeling as he stepped through one of the arched cellar windows. He moved slowly as if he stalked prey. He did not want to frighten away any new ideas that may enter his head.

"Well, you said treasure hunters come out here all the time," he finally spoke, turning to his counterparts. "Maybe he buried it here somewhere. Even *beneath* the cellar."

"You would think that over the decades, someone might have come across the jaguar already, and no one has ever reported finding anything," Reed said.

"And even if it is down there somewhere, we didn't bring any sonar or even shovels," Tim added. "Jimbo, I don't think it's here, dude."

James's back was to his cohorts. He stood as a cast-iron statue with his hands on his hips. Only his head moved from side to side, deep in thought over the journey until that moment. He became part of the scenery—property of the ruins itself. He turned to a monolith of contemplation, yet began to crack with the pressure of frustration that built from within.

"Goddamn it!" He swung around to face his colleagues at the façade of the ruins. "All this shit we've been through. Mugged. My house invaded and tossed. Secret societies. And we come up with nothing. Nothing!" he unloaded as Reed and Tim stood silent, reluctant to speak. "The idea that we might find something so historically relevant was so exciting. And now it's just shot to shit. All this we've been through. Fucking pointless."

In a burst of rage, he hunched over, quickly scooped up half of a broken red brick, and almost in one motion, hurled it forward, sending his friends to reel in the sudden appearance of a large object thrown their way. But he did not throw it randomly. His target was the back side of the concrete steps.

The brick cut through the air as it tumbled end over end, its incongruent broken sides tripping through the breeze like a miniature meteor on a collision course with an unknowing Earth. It struck the flat back of the concrete steps in slow motion, but did not shatter into red clay shards or bounce to the ground. Instead, it plunged into the concrete as small pieces of cement and gravel fired away from the point of impact as it disappeared into the structure.

"What the hell?" James perplexed as he hunched over and moved closer to examine what happened.

"What?" Tim edged closer, followed by Dr. Reed.

"Look at this." James drew slowly closer to the hole in the back of the stairs. "The friggin' brick punched right through," he puffed in disbelief as the other two approached.

"Maybe it's just not very well made," Dr. Reed suggested.

Tim ran his fingertips around the uneven rim of the hole made by the brick. Small grains of cement ground and stuck to his skin. He brushed the sandy grit from his fingers by rubbing them against his thumb. James then knocked at various points on the flat surface to listen for hollowness.

"Jimbo," Tim laughed, "it's not drywall. You're not going to get the hollow sound. But I can tell you that the concrete around this hole is way thinner than it should be."

"And look at this." Reed leaned in, but then took a step back. "You can faintly see a slightly indented rectangular shape around that hole."

"No shit." James stepped back. "How did I not see this before?" He looked around at the two other men. "What do you think?"

"I think," Tim said as he picked up another brick fragment, "it's time to vandalize a historic landmark." He walked up to the hole and beat the brick against the concrete as he chipped away at the edges of the present hole, ever widening it until most of the space within the subtle rectangular shape was absent.

"That's easy enough," James said with a grin. "Looks sturdy and unassuming, but accessible if Laffite needed to get something out."

"And let us hope he didn't," Reed added. "So which one of you is going to reach into the dark and mysterious hole?"

James could feel his heart rate increase just looking at the hole. His palms grew moist and his mouth dried out. *God only knows what kind of creepy spiders and shit might be in there.*

"All you, man," James firmly placed his hand on Tim's shoulder. "I reached into the last shadowy hole."

"Seriously?" he replied in shock. "Are you sure you don't want to be the one who uncovers an important piece of history?"

"Been there. Go for it."

Excitement became hesitation in Tim, with fluctuation between the two. He stared into another dimension. His fingers moved closer and trembled. Blackness yawned within the concrete vault and still concealed its contents. But his hands finally disappeared, dyed with the darkness momentarily.

The two other professors remained spellbound; awaiting what treasure or lack thereof would emerge from the depths. Breaths seemed to slow and scratch their throats. Eyes widened and pupils expanded for extra light. James felt his hands move toward the opening in the back of the staircase as if to use telekinesis to will his friend's hand to grasp the contents and return to the light.

"Oh shit," Tim gasped with a start to his colleagues.

"What? What?" James's heart fluttered with worry.

"I've got something. I freakin' feel something. It feels like a box or case."

His hands firmly pressed against dust-coated wood, and then he gripped it. He closed his eyes and breathed deeply before he retracted his hands and the vaulted time capsule with exhale. Sunlight washed over the wooden box for the first time in nearly two centuries to expose its caramel wood tones to the longing eyes of the three academics. The layer of dust caked atop long, thin planks that formed a miniature treasure chest.

"No lock or latch." Tim ran his index finger along the edge where the lid met the front side, and then shuffled loose the dust that had accumulated on his skin.

Each of the men simply stared at the box and then made brief eye contact with one another. Perhaps the box contained something different. Maybe there was a worthless old hat. It could hold doubloons, and as exciting as that would be, it would not be overly profound. It could be worse. It could contain nothing.

"Oh, just open the goddamned thing!" Reed blurted in frustration.

His temper's mercury fell as quickly as it had risen. He grinned with embarrassment, his eyes closed and the corners of his mouth curled upward with the astonished gazes from his colleagues. As his aged, loose face continued to glow red, James and Tim returned their attention to the old box.

James reached for the lid of the old chest as it still rested within Tim's hands. Tim even angled the front of it his way so he could have easier access. He held his breath as he lifted the weighty lid and carefully flipped it back to expose the interior.

Within, a dingy gray cotton cloth was crumpled and wadded, packed into the small confines as bubble wrap would a Christmas present from Grandma. James positioned his hands to the edges of the box between the wood and the cloth and worked them carefully into the interior until he had a grasp on the concealed object. It certainly had weight and mass. He first misjudged how heavy it might be. But within a moment, he lifted the wrapped object upward until it had fully been removed, and then he pulled it to himself to almost become one with it.

Four eagerly fixed eyes waited without blinking, paralyzed by suspense. James, still crouched with Tim beside the opened staircase vault, set the object upon his left knee. He peeled away the cloth from the middle, and unfolded the heavy spring flower as petals out from the pistil. Yet, it would bring forth no wondrous fragrance or nectar for the bees. Perhaps it brought knowledge and power, which smells sweeter still.

With each fold removed, the object became more exposed. It was gray, cold, and lifeless. There upon James's knee, atop the fully unfolded cloth, lay a figurine of a regal jungle cat the size of a child's doll. It was perfectly preserved. There were no chips, cracks, or imperfections in its carving. It was not worn as if to have been handled often. It was a cold, smooth, light gray piece of solid stone, carved into the likeness of a sitting jaguar. Its back was upright and front paws up while two menacing fangs descended from its mouth.

"Amazing," Reed uttered in a stupor.

"Limestone," Tim said as he examined and pointed to a section of the figurine. "Typical stone used in Mayan temples."

Reed and Tim were ecstatic, like two kids with a new toy, but James's expression never changed. He lifted the statue and held it with both hands at an angle before him. His eyes were affixed, it seemed, permanently to it. He did not blink or smile. He gazed into the thing's very soul, entranced as smiles upon his friends' faces turned to concern.

"James," Tim attempted. "Jimbo! Snap out of it!"

"Sorry." James blinked and shook his head. "Just thinking about, well, I don't know."

"There's something else in the chest," Reed pointed.

Tim, still holding the old box, reached inside to retrieve three aged yellowish pages from within. They were crisp and unfolded, yet had an uneven left edge that indicated they had been torn from a bound book of some sort.

"It's in Spanish," Tim said with a closer look.

"The captain's log from the galleon the British took it from." James remembered the Laffite papers.

"Let's see," Tim began. "El capitan is writing about inventory—boring, boring, boring. Ooh, a flogging! Cool," he continued, mouthing words silently as he went. He turned the page, and finally grew a bit more excited. "Hey, here it is. The captain says they had just returned from an expedition into the jungle through British Honduras—now Belize—and into their own territory of Guatemala. It was some sort of special mission to the island city the locals called Noh Peten."

"Insurrection? Stopping a rebellion?" James suggested.

"According to this log, they were looking for a totem of some sort. A totem with myths and writings."

"A stela," Reed said. "They're all over the Mayan lands."

"Well, this says they copied the writings from the stela and took from the elders a jaguar statue that they valued greatly—they had to even kill a few locals who tried to stop them." He went to the next page. "And look, there are the hieroglyphs."

"I wonder what it says," James puzzled. "Instruction manual? Myth? It had to have been important. I can't read this crap, though."

"Me neither." Tim shook his head. "But we know someone who can."

"Matt Davidson," James said. "Still lives in Baton Rouge. Oh Jesus, you haven't seen him in a while, have you? Uh-oh."

"What?" Tim asked.

"Long story—I'll tell you later," James replied. "Right now, let's get the hell out of here before the cops catch us trespassing."

"That's probably a good idea," Reed agreed as he watched the other two men slowly arise from a squat with the increasingly common groans of a man who inched toward middle age. "I'm just not looking forward to scaling that fence again." He bent over and inserted a finger into the hole in his trousers.

The other men bubbled with a deep, meaty chuckle. The sight of this old man catching his pants on the spiked top of the metal fence was hilarious in a demented, voyeuristic sort of way. They should feel bad for him. He was a good bit older, so what if he broke a hip?

"Maybe you don't have to." James glanced to the front of the property, and pointed that way with a smile of disbelief.

"Oh bollocks." Reed rolled his eyes at the sight of a small gate that separated the forgotten lot from the sidewalk and bustling harbor-side highway.

"How did we not notice that before?" Tim burst with laughter. "Three grown men with PhDs and none of us noticed!"

"It's locked, though." Reed tried to make himself feel better.

"You'll find that's not a problem for Jim here," Tim chuckled as James had already extracted his wallet from his back pocket and moved toward the gate.

In a natural set of motions, as if he were retrieving cash, he removed the tension bar and "snake" pick from one of the compartments. He crouched toward the ground to analyze the type of lock and found it to be the most ordinary of padlocks that secured a simple aluminum latch.

"Piece of cake," he said, and placed the short end of the L-shaped bar into the keyhole and then raked the pins until the bar ejected from the base. "Got it." He pivoted on the balls of his feet with a smile, but as he looked beyond his friends and the old cellar, he was stricken with a stampeding herd of fear. "Look out!"

The warning was not timely enough. Reed and Tim had barely registered and processed the words, unable to yet react. Two rapid bursts of concrete dust erupted from the old above-ground cellar walls, which left craters as the dust cleared. They accompanied no menacing muzzle pops; only the metallic sound of the moving slide of a semi-automatic handgun. They knew what was happening without turning to look for the origin, yet they did anyway.

At the back of the property where the three professors had jumped the fence were two men. The taller man's arm lifted again with another silenced bullet from the elongated barrel extension across the lot, and again into the concrete wall to their right. The short, squat, balding man to his right hurriedly struggled to hoist himself over the treacherous aluminum spikes at the top of the chain-link fence.

Reed and Tim bent their knees and arched their backs forward as their hands lifted to cover their heads. They hastily moved and leaped through the window holes of the cellar walls, and then ran for the newly open gate with all the strength and power that their leg muscles could muster.

The fat attacker in the back of the lot fell over the fence and rolled on the grass like a wayward child's ball. Shirt and pants torn, he fought his own shape and weight to lift himself to his feet only to join his partner in gazing across the lot at the escaping professors.

"They're getting away, Rupert!" Nick yelled at his partner just to the other side of the fence.

"Bugger!" Rupert looked up from his position on the grass, and then he scurried clumsily to his feet to scale the fence again.

The light aluminum construction was old, and swayed with the weight of the short, stout man. He lost his footing as he attempted to cross to the other side, and toppled over head-first to catch his pants on the spikes at the top. He hung there inverted, partially on the back of his neck and shoulders while the aluminum spikes clung invasively to his faded denim jeans.

"You idiot!" Nick threw his hands into the air, and fired impatient looks at his cohort and down the dusty lane to his right. "The damned gate in the front is open!"

Rupert struggled as he flailed around in his awkward position like a freshly-caught fish on the end of some angler's hook. He frantically pulled at his pant leg. Suddenly, there was a brief rip and then the rest of the denim toward his foot tore around the circumference of his leg to leave frayed white cotton threads that swayed with the wind. He leapt to his feet and into an immediate sprint with his partner down the dusty alley between the small businesses on the block. Dust kicked up from the backs of their casual leather boots like some old cartoon.

"Unbelievable," Rupert panted as he ran. "These are my favorite jeans."

"Just pray they don't get away, lard-ass," Nick responded with fury.

James and Tim quickly approached the silver SUV with Reed lagging a bit behind. James tugged and pulled at the cluster of keys inside his right front pocket. The keys clinked together like Christmas bells with a yank from their denim prison, and with a thumb to the rubber-buttoned remote, the locks of the vehicle clicked open. Tim ripped open the passenger door, followed by James climbing hastily behind the wheel.

"Dr. Reed," Tim screamed as he saw the unknown attackers emerge from the lot ahead of them. "Hurry!"

The top-center of the windshield spider-webbed with cracks, accompanied by a pop and the sudden appearance of a hole at the center of the pattern. The back right door flung open, and Reed leapt inside. He slammed it behind him as James cranked the engine. He could see the two men more closely now that they approached the Tahoe and the street. The taller man with the gun no longer took aim at them, but they attempted to rush the vehicle. He yanked down the gear shift like an antique slot machine arm, and then stomped on the accelerator as he cut the wheel. Tim could see the shorter man grow dangerously close before the SUV fully began moving. As Rupert reached for the handle, Tim pulled the chrome door latch and kicked open the door with enough force, added to the vehicle's motion, to send the man lifted from his feet and then flat onto the pavement.

"Everybody okay?" James labored, nearly unable to take in full breaths.

"Jesus!" Reed's sweaty face turned to the rear window. "They bloody shot at us! Who were those people?" he burst, the adrenaline apparent in his voice.

"Society of the Lost Dominion, I'd imagine," Tim yelled.

The Tahoe squealed around the residential block at a highly illegal speed as it cornered back around to Harborside Drive. James's eyes did not waver from his straight-forward beaming look. He focused on the industrial shipyard across the busy highway, oblivious to the passing vehicles. His foot, a petrified tree trunk, found root upon the gas pedal. He increased his speed as he cut the wheel to the right ahead of swerving cars on the street. A medley of differently-pitched horns formed together into a power chord of road rage, yet James gripped the wheel as if he would strangle it while he weaved in and out of lanes and ran red traffic lights.

"Thank God." James exhaled as if he had been holding his breath for several minutes. "Lost 'em."

"I don't think so." Reed turned to the rear window and watched a small, white two-door coupe pass cars at break-neck speed.

"I hope no one left anything at the hotel." James stomped again on the gas. "I'm going to try to take a less congested street," he said as he glanced into the rearview mirror. He then sharply turned right and skidded away from the busy Harborside Drive and an immediate left at the next street.

"That's not a street, James!" Tim instinctively used his arms to brace himself between the seat at his back and the dashboard before him. "That's a horseshoe drive."

"Oh shit." James's eyes nearly shot from within their sockets as he approached the dead end, unable to stop with the pursuing gunmen. "What is this place?" He looked around at the acres of clustered multiple-level buildings that surrounded them.

"UT Medical Complex," Tim read the sign.

"Great." James scowled as he quickly decided what he was going to do next. "Hang on." He narrowed his eyes and stepped on the accelerator, much to the horror of his passengers.

The Tahoe struck the low concrete curb at a small space between two parked cars. The shocks became pogo sticks as the heavy vehicle went slightly airborne and came back down onto the campus walkways of concrete and red clay pavers.

"Palm tree," Tim shouted, horrified and reeling into the fetal position within the leather bucket seat.

The sport coupe behind them lost its plastic front end as it jumped the same curb in pursuit. James veered around the palm tree ahead, and with the dead end courtyard in the near distance, swerved ninety degrees to the right to leave a trail of black marks on the nicely-kept walkway.

"Move! Move!" James screamed at the pedestrians as if they could hear him, all the while motioning them to do so as he sped forward.

He did not relinquish the pressure he placed on the pedal and streaked across campus with the coupe in pursuit. Doctors in lab coats dove to the side as charts and paperwork launched into a haphazard pile upon the ground. Nurses tripled the force they used to push the sick patients around in wheelchairs, moving clear of the Tahoe's destructive path. A very sick old woman who strolled in the sun with her mobile IV still linked to her veins simply stopped, petrified as the two automobiles raced past her close enough for the disturbed air to tug her hospital gown to the side.

James spied his exit ahead and raced into the latter part of a circle drive that led into the street. Another bullet punctured the back hatch of the SUV as he veered left and again headed east for Ferry Road. He did not even touch the brake and blasted through every last intersection, despite stop signs and traffic lights. He finally steered left onto Ferry Road and the palms on the boulevard blurred by them as they headed for the ferry.

"There's a line to get on the ferry." Reed pointed ahead, and then swiveled his head to the rear to confirm they were still being followed.

"We cannot be on the same ferry with these assholes," Tim said.

The Tahoe slowed as they approached the line that formed before the pay booths for the ferry. His eyes, partially concealed by his lowered brow, rattled rapidly from side to side as if in some kind of lucid dream-like state.

"James," Tim began calmly, and then became more frantic. "James! What are we doing?"

James smashed the pedal beneath his feet. He cut sharply to the right and rocketed around the line for the ferry, and then down an access street separate from the ferry area. They flew along the two-lane street to the side of the ferry line as he watched the slowly-moving vehicles pass to his left. Finally, he saw a small break in the line. In one hesitation-free motion, James veered over the low curb and into a small, empty space in front of the next car to get on the ferry. He stopped abruptly with almost no indication to anyone around of what had just happened. The only people that seemed to notice were the ones in the car James had skipped in front of, and as they cursed and blew their horns, the Tahoe pulled safely up the ramp and parked while the gate closed.

"You're calling the council and explaining—not me," Nick said to his worried partner as they sat at a standstill in line for the ferry.

Aboard, the ferry's engines rumbled and the water churned behind the vessel. It inched forward in its journey to carry passengers across from the island back to the Bolivar Peninsula. James, without a word, opened the door and jumped out of the vehicle, headed for the edge of the deck. Tim and Reed, physically exhausted, exited the SUV and started for the edge as well, watching James lean his back against the waist-level wall to light a cigarette right next to the "No Smoking" sign.

"What now?" Tim walked up, his hands in his pockets and his posture slouched.

"Get to Matt's in Baton Rouge," James said as he exhaled the noxious cloud of satisfying smoke. "But first I'm calling Noelle."

"I'd better call the misses, as well." Reed smiled and then removed the dated phone from his pocket, opened it, and began dialing as he walked away.

"I thought you were divorced," Tim turned with perplexity.

"Um, oh yes," Reed clarified. "But I do have a girlfriend back home." He then continued with his call, and roamed away for privacy.

Through glass panes, pastel blue skies were dotted with light puffs of white cloud that moved lazily inland from the gulf. Heavy concrete pylons rose above the murky water and served as rest stops for brown pelicans that took a break from fishing on the water. Industry mingled with nature. Oil platforms rested near estuaries. Barges lumbered by, dancing with lofty seagulls that trailed the wake in hope that the propellers would churn up some minnows or even shrimp.

"Yes sir." Rupert's eyes and brow were of a dog reprimanded over urinating on the carpet. "I do apologize, Chancellor," he spoke again into the cell phone. "We won't fail again." He nodded silently again, and then looked to Nick, who sat in the driver's seat. "Nick? Yes, sir. He's right here."

Nick had been silent since the ferry left. He propped his chin upon his hand, lost in his own thoughts. He stared blankly through the window to his left as he watched the sights of the port, but did not really watch it. He heard his name and turned as his colleague handed the phone over to him.

"Sir?" Nick sighed as he rubbed his eyes and forehead with his fingers and thumb. "I apologize, sir," he replied after the red-hot voice in the receiver chastised the two men. "It shall not happen again. The next information we receive on their whereabouts, we will take custody of the statue. I personally guarantee it."

Ill thoughts and deep contemplation flowed from his head into his fingertip. He listened for another moment, and then with a lazy, self-ashamed motion, pressed the button to end the call. He hung his head for a moment and stared at his lap. He then lifted his chin to stare forth at the ferry-less dock. In his mind, he envisioned the future attack, even if it meant they had to trail the professors the full distance back to New Orleans.

Chapter 11

Ahead moved an endless stretch of gray bordered by parallel walls of green and an azure ceiling. It was a multicolored tube that stretched on forever with no sight of the beginning or end. Occasionally, a break would occur in the forest and swampy murals beyond the shoulder, and the professors could see a small country home or a dingy truck-stop frequented by the tanker drivers who hauled gasoline and diesel from the Lake Charles refineries to the rest of the region.

Tim lounged in the back, his seatbelt unbuckled. His phone plugged in, his world was now digital. He was unattainable from the outside. Dr. Reed had fallen prey to the straight, flat interstate that gushed forth to him. His eyes were glazed. Forgotten were the perils he had experienced only hours before. His mouth hung ajar as he appeared blank in his forward stare.

James, however, thought actively as he listened to the air whistle through the bullet holes in the windshield. He had trouble quieting the perpetual screams within. They kept him up at night. He longed to turn it off. But those thoughts churned on, an endless need to understand.

"So does Matty know we're coming?" Tim, still glued to his phone, spoke suddenly.

"Yeah, I texted him from the ferry," James replied.

"He's still teaching at LSU, right? I guess he didn't go out of town for spring break."

"No," James giggled a little. "He certainly wouldn't have gone out of town."

"What?" Tim implored, almost agitated. "What's the deal with Matt? I'm dying here."

"Okay, okay . . ." James, still smiling, composed himself to explain. "He still teaches at LSU, but has arranged with the university to do so via web conferencing and teaching assistants. Office hours are done by phone."

"Jesus, is he homebound or something?" Tim gasped. "What happened?" He brimmed with concern.

"A few years ago, Matt was robbed at gunpoint just north of campus."

"By our old stomping grounds?"

"Pretty close-by," James replied, and then continued. "Anyway, some guy robbed him for his wallet, watch, and shoes, and then pistol-whipped him across the forehead."

"Christ," Tim grimaced.

"Yeah, and now he's afraid to leave the house."

"So he's agoraphobic. He's lucky the university was able to be flexible with his employment."

"Well, he went there for his undergrad degree, his master's and his doctorate, so I guess when you give a school enough money, they'll let you pretty much do anything but change the name of the stadium. Not to mention he's one of the country's foremost experts on Mayan language and culture."

"I hate to interrupt you gentlemen," Dr. Reed said, "but I'm afraid I have to stop at a petrol station."

"Again?" James rolled his eyes. "We've stopped five times already just since we got off of Galveston Ferry."

"I told you not to get that huge bottle of water back in Beaumont," Tim jabbed.

"I'm sorry," Reed said, humbled, but firmly. "I'm an old man with a swelling prostate. It makes me have to stop frequently for a *jimmy riddle*, and then when I begin to go, it takes forever."

"Did you just say 'jimmy riddle' in describing having to piss?" James laughed, somehow less agitated now. "Fine," he said after a moment, "I'll find a gas station. I probably need to fill up anyway. But you have to make it as quick as your swollen prostate will allow. I shouldn't need to remind you of the gun-toting assholes likely following us."

"Understood, sir," Reed smiled.

Southwest Louisiana was sparse for populated exits along I-10. Most exits led off onto a rural highway that would lead to some tiny Cajun village somewhere off the beaten path. It might lead you back into the bayous and boat launches of Acadiana where you should find extraordinary cooking and a bathroom to use, but it may be miles away. It took at least ten minutes to find a quasi-suitable gas station. Reed's right leg bounced rapidly as if he were on amphetamines. His loose, wrinkled facial skin clenched and contorted with the pressure in his bladder. The pavement on the exit ramp was bumpy and masticated with shoddy patch jobs, which made it even worse for the old professor.

As James pulled into the decayed gas station, the Tahoe bounced over uneven asphalt of variable darkness and freshness. Both double-sided pumps were free of customers and only the sole employee's battered and unmaintained little coupe gave indication that the store was operational. The windows and signs were a faded version of their once new brilliance. Now they were covered in thin sheets of grayish fungi and road dust. It was a crumbling bit of Americana set against a thick backdrop of deep green foliage.

The Tahoe stopped beside one of the pumps as three doors opened almost simultaneously. Dr. Reed wasted no time to scurry off into the shack of a convenience store without a word. James stepped out and walked back to fill the SUVs gas tank. He opened the cover and unscrewed the black plastic cap, and allowed it to hang from its lanyard.

"I'm going in for a bag of chips or something," Tim half-yelled from the other side of the vehicle as he backpedalled toward the store.

James said nothing in reply, and continued to start the pump by sliding his card into the payment slot. *It's amazing these little stations even have these. I always expect to have to crank the damned thing this far out in the boondocks.* The outdated electronic banner indicated an approval, so he inserted the nozzle into the tank and set the lever to allow the flow of fuel to continue as he walked away. *I'd better go take a piss, too. I don't want to have to go later and be a hypocrite.* He pulled his keys from his pocket and mashed the rubber button on the SUV's remote control and listened to the horn honk once as he approached the store.

The smell of oil and gasoline rode the wind currents of warm air like schools of migrant jellyfish. James strode across the oil-blotted concrete, littered with flattened cigarette butts. As he approached the smudged and filthy double doors, he pulled and entered the store where it was somewhat warmer and stuffier than outside. No air moved inside, except for the small white plastic fan behind the counter. There, a young, greasy clerk sat perched upon a stool with a monthly low-rider enthusiast magazine in his hand. His logoed work shirt was unwashed and his short hair was slicked forward atop buzzed sides. A smudged-on mustache was orbited by current acne and the scars of pimples past. *I know that look*, James smiled at his half-shut eyes. *Hangovers are a bitch. Or is he just high?* But he shrugged and moved for the restroom.

He strode across the synthetic tiles. He passed Tim on the next aisle, who rummaged through various bags of chips and brands of beef jerky as he tried to make a decision on how he would complete his daily fat and salt intake in one sitting. James kept moving, now able to feel the pressure in his bladder. He reached for the knob and attempted to turn it, but it would not budge. *Shit, that's Reed, I guess. Still going?* He moved his ear closer to the door. *Is he talking in there?* James puzzled. *Is he on the phone? Or is his talking to his penis? Never mind. I'm a guy. I'll go piss out back.*

With that, he walked back down the candy aisle, unnoticed by Tim or even the clerk behind the counter. With urgency in his bladder, James turned the corner and did not even stop as he pushed through the doors and around the side of the building. He stepped carefully through the wasteland of plastic and glass shards and dodged fire ant mounds and anonymous pieces of rusted steel that had met demise years ago. He finally found his place along the concrete walls, obscured from the road and parking lot, and started to relieve himself.

He finished with a shake and zip, and trekked back to the Tahoe. His eyes were still on the deadly, littered, weed-infested ground when he came to the corner of the store. As he lifted his head, he first noticed that another car had parked on the other side of the pump from his SUV. A man walked toward the store, while the other passenger exited the small, white coupe, but stayed near the pump. First, there were no apprehensions, but then came a stabbing epiphany, accompanied by banshees of panic in waves that made his skin turn cold and his stomach rumble. He recognized the coupe and the two men who had stepped out of it.

James stopped his advance in protective reflex, and retreated back around the corner. He thought quickly, his mind flooded with solutions that all seemed to fall short. Still panicked, he scanned about for something, though he did not know what. An escape route? A weapon? Then something caught his eye, and it inspired. He crouched down and reached for a rubber-handled flat-head screwdriver that had been abandoned and blanketed in rust. He grasped it in his hand, stood, and then peered around the corner to see that the short, stout man had stepped up on the back running board of the SUV. His upper torso was inside the back of the vehicle through the shot-out window, while the pudgy lower half of his body hung helplessly out.

This asshole's trying to get the jaguar, James thought as he trotted quickly but stealthily toward the front of the Tahoe and then around the pump. He crouched to the side and checked to see that he was unnoticed by the man he saw enter the store and the man who rifled through the SUV. He then duck-walked to each tire of the white coupe, lifted the screwdriver high above his head, and plunged it murderously into the rubber to release the air inside.

Nick, the spike-headed Englishman yanked the door open and swooshed into the store. His head darted to the left only to see no one there. He moved his eyes to the clerk with a lift of his right eyebrow. The clerk did not even look up. The only other man was Tim, who was oblivious, caught in a debate between Cheetos and TGI Fridays Potato Skins. Nick did not recognize him, only having seen the men he had been chasing for a brief moment in Galveston. But he knew there was only one vehicle out there and its back window was shot out.

With that thought, he turned his shoulders and head to the left behind him to see his cohort's hind end stuck out of the back of the SUV like Winnie the Pooh. He shook his head, returned his attention to the man on the chip aisle, and idly browsed the magazines near the door. He only saw the one man, which worried him. He was sure there were three. Perhaps they were both in the restroom, but he was not sure if it was a multiple-toilet washroom or a single-holer. He checked the car in the front again for any sign of the other professors, but only saw Rupert. It did not matter if he saw the other men as long as he kept everyone at bay in the store long enough for his partner to gain possession of the jaguar.

He inched his way ever closer to the bathrooms to the far right of the store, now directly behind Tim on the parallel aisle. His heart pounded within his ribcage like it would burst. He continued to pretend to shop, yet frequently lifted his cold blue eyes to check the scene.

The squeal of a door hinge punctured the silence. Nick's instinct overtook him and he reached around to the small of his back to retrieve his weapon and pointed it in the direction of the restroom without even looking to see who it was. There emerged Dr. Reed, who caught sight of the menacing muzzle and stopped immediately.

Dr. Reed stood motionless as Tim finally looked up from the Cheetos he had selected. He saw the old professor stationary and staring in an odd direction. There was no fear in his eyes or tremble in his hands. His arms hung to the sides weighted by nearly numb, blood-gorged fingers. His heart pulsed within them, yet at a calm rate. In his face was a coldness and even hatred of unknown cause. Only a second or so passed. There stood a tall man with a handgun pointed at Reed. Roles were reversed. Reed showed no fear, yet the gunman, though steady, beamed terror in his eyes. But that terror was only momentary as Nick sighted Tim from the corner of his left eye, and immediately retargeted.

The gunman spun to the left with no hesitation. Tim dropped instantly to the dirty linoleum floor as a few shots whooshed from the silencer into the glass soda cooler behind him. Plastic bottles burst with dark cara-mel-colored blood that pooled and fizzed on the floor as Tim scurried around the end of the aisle by the beef jerky as the clerk, who had finally put down his magazine, cowered behind the counter. Nick moved slowly in the opposite direction around the other end near Dr. Reed.

"What do you want from us, you hooligan?" Reed yelled angrily, his hands raised and backing up as the younger gunman slowly approached. "Who are you? You coward!"

Rupert could hear the ruckus inside, and stopped his struggle and search for the statue. He looked through the back right window at a tinted view of the convenience store and could see Nick with his gun drawn.

"Perfect. Goddamned perfect." He hurriedly pushed himself from out of the back window, prepared to draw his gun and go in to help.

He plopped heavily to the ground, a shock delivered to his feet as he landed. It took him a moment to balance and find composure, and when he did, something else caught his attention. James had appeared between the Tahoe and the pump, and he was smiling, armed with the gas nozzle. Before Rupert could produce his weapon, James applied pressure to the nozzle's handle, and sprayed a noxious, fuming stream of gasoline through the air. The light waved and refracted along the air-borne stream as if the liquid produced shock waves. It found its mark as it doused the squat Englishman and burned his eyes.

James dropped the nozzle and struggled to pull the keys from his pocket, finally able to unlock his vehicle. He yanked on the handle and hopped inside in one motion, and then cranked the engine.

Nick, distracted by the old professor's yelling and then the cranking engine, looked into the parking lot. For that brief moment, Tim had his opportunity. He grasped a heavy, dust-coated can of chili from the bottom shelf and stood erect. The can and Tim's hand looped overhead with increasing velocity and then the projectile flew freely across the aisles. It cracked against the back of Nick's head and a reflex shot fired into the ceiling before he slumped unconsciously on the floor.

"Let's go." The old professor scurried and hopped over the man on the floor.

"I want to see who the hell he is." Tim, with all the fury his sympathetic nervous system could muster, knelt by the man and dug into his back pocket. He removed a wallet, and then opened it to find a London-issued driver's license. "Nicholas David Logan-Reed." He dropped the wallet upon hearing James honk the horn outside.

The two men rushed through the door as quickly as they could. They could see the little fat man writhe in pain. Behind them, they could hear the doors open again. Their hearts sunk at the thought that they might still be gunned down, yet they kept running for the SUV. Tim briefly looked over his shoulder to see a very angry man who held a gun pointed in their direction. *Oh God, this is it.*

"Wait!" Rupert yelled to Nick. "Don't shoot!"

Nick stopped and observed the situation. He could see Rupert was doused in something and could see the fumes fill the air. He caught sight of the hose hanging and nozzle at the pump. Then he knew why he was begged not to shoot.

"Damn it." Nick stomped as he lowered his weapon and he watched the men climb into the SUV and drive off. As soon as the Tahoe had left the parking lot, Nick ran out to Rupert who still struggled to open his eyes fully. "Get in the damned car, Rupert," he screamed as he ran up to the little coupe, but before he even reached for the door handle, he noticed the roof was a bit lower than before. He looked down at the tires and saw that they had been flattened. His shoulders slunk and emotion drained from his face.

"This keeps happening," Tim struggled for breath. "They keep finding us. We have got to get rid of this truck."

"Agreed." James mashed the pedal to the floor. "Baton Rouge is just over an hour away. Let's haul ass and hit a car rental place."

Chapter 12

Leaves crumpled and soil was tamped beneath heavy, powerful feet. They moved with both agility and force. Shockwaves seemed to ripple from each step. They stopped as four legs flexed and bulged with wild, natural muscle beneath black-spotted golden fur. Shoulder bones jutted upward as the dangerous and beautiful cat crouched closer to the moist ground shaded by the canopy above. Benevolent in his nature, his face remained soft and his eyes innocently studying. But in an instant, those legs sprang and the jaguar moved forward with god-like power. His mouth widened to reveal his menacing fangs as he descended upon his prey.

James's eyes popped open to see only the beige material that upholstered the ceiling of his SUV. Sweat rolled in steady streams down his temple and stubbled cheeks as he uncrossed his arms and sat up in the leather seat. He looked around, unsure at first where he was, and breathed a sigh of relief as he came to his senses.

"Okay there, boss?" Tim glanced over from the driver's seat.

"Um," he paused groggily. "Um, yeah. How long was I out?" He looked out the window to see the steel supports of the bridge pass rapidly and the lazy old Mississippi River stretch to the north and south.

"About an hour."

"Geez." James shook his head as he tried to physically fling away the remnants of his nap.

"I think you needed that," Tim said.

"Yeah. Freakin' . . . Freakin' weird dream. We find a rental car place?"

"Yeah, up on College Drive. We'll ditch this piece of shit and head over to Matty's."

The landmarks of their riverside alma mater brought forth brief snippets of fond memories from a bygone era, which faded as quickly as the scenery as they entered the curvy, narrow interstate highways of Baton Rouge. Tim pressed the brake to slow down among the ravenous drivers in his company, anxiety now a part of the experience. A blur of trees and residences turned into the broad, picturesque university lakes. But in a flash, that too was gone, and was replaced by gaudy signs for restaurants and bars that adorned a crumbling concrete shell of commercialism.

Soon, he signaled and changed lanes to follow the loopy exit down to College Drive. They stopped with the long line of vehicles held up by the traffic light that dictated access to the street. It was a bustle, as usual, with an immense amount of traffic made up of unyielding, unhappy motorists who made their way home from work. The light clicked green, and the line edged forward as Tim and the professors barely were able to make their left onto College Drive. Soon, they pulled into the rental car lot to park among a detailed and polished fleet affront an aged building.

"Be right with you," a droll, uninterested voice sounded as the men opened and entered.

The sole visible employee available stood with lazy posture behind the counter as his belly bulged beneath the crisp button-down and tie. His greasy, wavy hair was complemented perfectly by a snake's smile and the emergence of a shade of a mustache above his lip. His eyes were set on the small plastic screen he held before his face as he feverishly tapped at the virtual keyboard with his thumbs until he sent his message and turned his attention to the waiting gentlemen.

"What can I do for you?" he addressed the customers.

"The obvious," James said as they strode up to the counter.

"Okay." The salesman shrugged, a dumb, blank look on his face that begged more information. "So what do you want?"

"To rent a car," James reiterated as his face glared with the obvious.

"Okay." The salesman shrugged again. "What kind? Sedan? SUV? Minivan? Sports car?"

"Shit, I don't know. Just a car. Economy car."

"Okay," he said, a little more satisfied.

"Economy car?" Tim protested. "For the three of us? I am not sitting in the back of some shitty little coupe with a cramp in my ass while we drive all over God's green Earth."

"Well what do you want, a damned Escalade?" James argued.

"We have one," the salesman interjected, though no one acknowledged.

"No, just don't get the smallest thing on the lot just because you're a cheapskate," Tim said.

"Just get another Tahoe," Reed suggested.

"No," James and Tim said in unison.

"Get the same kind of vehicle?" James added. "Are you nuts? We need a completely different look."

"But not some little hatchback," Tim argued.

"We have a Chrysler sedan," the salesman said. "Brand new. Black. Full-size. It should be plenty of room." His eyes widened as he wondered about these three and their intentions. "A little more inconspicuous."

"But black?" James rebutted. "Like a government vehicle. Looks like someone important would be in it. You have it in silver?"

"How would a copper-ish color work?" the salesman suggested.

"Fine, ring it up," James conceded.

"You got it." He began typing away at the keyboard behind the cheap blue counter. His fingers rhythmically danced with corresponding plastic clicks. "Payment?" He stopped and accepted James's debit card, rang it, and handed it back. A few more seconds of typing and the printer beneath the counter sprang to life to finally present a set of contractual agreements that James was to sign and agree to. "See this?" He pointed with a pen. "This says you agree to use the car for a rate of forty-nine dollars a day until you return it. You can keep it for seven days without renewing, but beyond that, you must renew. Here is the insurance charge in case you have an accident. And this stuff . . . yadda, yadda, yadda . . . Oh yeah, and no smoking or off-roading or anything. Just don't bring it back all nasty or they'll Jew you over for the cleaning fee."

The three men looked up from the monotony of contract and agreement jargon, awakened by the rare slur used in a public, professional setting. They simply stared at the man in shock as he continued to roll through all the points in the contract until he finally stopped and turned his attention to the customers. He scanned their faces and found new expressions before he suddenly realized what was happening.

"Oh, guys. It's okay. I'm Jewish."

The professors just glanced at one another and shrugged as the young salesman trotted off to the back, fumbled with some keys that jingled in the case on the wall, and then returned with the right set. James signed the agreement, nodded, and accepted the keys. They then turned, and without a word exited to find the right car.

"I see it," Tim said, and gestured ahead. "Right over there."

"So what about the Tahoe?" Reed glanced over at the badly maimed SUV at the far end of the parking lot.

"Just leave it," James said as they continued to approach the rental car. "I'll get Noelle to come pick it up after we figure all this out. Her mother's isn't far from here."

"Here we go." Tim got into the car after James pressed the button to unlock it. "Let's see how Matt's ancient Mayan is these days."

Chapter 13

"Here it is." James stopped the new sedan along the curb.

The men peered out the window at a very charming one-story raised cottage with a nice little porch in the front. The yellow paint on the siding and the white of the trim was shiny and new. Two gabled windows peered out from among weathered, old-style shingles upon the steep creole slopes of the roof. The flowers bloomed in the hedges in front and along the driveway while the yard remained littered with the brown oak leaves left over from the fall.

They stepped out of the new car smell and into the warm, wet Baton Rouge air. With a short walk up the blackened concrete walkway, they stepped up onto the porch boards with a hollow resonance. James peeled back the screen door with a screech of the spring and knocked firmly on the glass inset of the solid main door. Under his arm was the box that held the stone jaguar and log papers. The professors cast their gazes in various directions, a strange nervousness present with the arrival at an unfamiliar place. They looked up the street and back down the other way. There was little traffic in the quiet, off-campus neighborhood. Busier highways and streets nearby bled over with their distant noise, but mostly it was peaceful.

A bump against the door caught their attention. Then there was a slight rustle. After a few moments, one deadbolt slid from its place in the door jam. Then came another, and another until four deadbolts were unlocked, plus a chain and the lock in the knob itself before it turned and the door opened. There, half cowering on the other side of the gray veil of the screen door, a rather tall man in flannel pajama pants and a plain white t-shirt eyed keenly the company that paid him a visit. Erratic, and almost confused, he bit his bottom lip as he examined the men, but finally smiled as widely as his eyes narrowed into slits.

"James," he burst. "And Tim! Shit, man, how have you been? It's been years." He pulled his old friend in for a nearly uncomfortable hug. "You guys some in." He stepped back as his slippers shuffled against the floorboards.

The air inside had an old smell, like that of the storage area of a library that kept all the deteriorating books in the collection. In the dim brownish light, the walls hung with history's knick-knacks. Spanish conquistador swords mingled with Incan masks. Images of Central American temples and rubbings of Mayan stellae took most of the wall space not claimed by cabinets of barely used china and endless bookshelves. A small table set as if Matt expected someone for dinner gathered dust, and had collected newspapers, magazines, and random objects. The shelves in the parlor library were overstuffed. Books of all sorts spilled over and lay in various locations. The kitchen, though modern and functional, was stuffed with dirty dishes, pans, and the general clutter and filth of dozens of meals cooked with no cleanup.

"Welcome, boys," he said as he led them inside.

"Jesus, you've got to get a maid, Matty," James chuckled.

"Yeah, I know. You'd think I'd have all the time in the world to clean with all the time I spend here. It's just too far gone at this point." He stopped for a moment, and then beamed again at Tim. "Damn, this brings back memories. So glad to have us all back in the same room together. And this is . . ." He motioned to Dr. Reed with the expectation that his friends would make the introduction.

"Oh yes," James sprang. "Yes, sorry. Dr. Matt Davidson, meet Dr. Rylan Reed, a professor at Oxford."

"Great to meet you." Matt shook the old professor's hand with enthusiasm. "You look familiar. Have we?"

"I don't think so," Reed replied. "But it is a pleasure to meet you."

"Hmm." Matt shrugged and began to lead the men back toward his study. "One of those faces."

"What is your specialty, Dr. Davidson?" Reed trailed James and Tim.

"Matt."

"What?" Reed asked, confused.

"Call me Matt. And I specialize in Mesoamerican native culture."

"Any particular area?"

"Oh, you know. Mayans, Olmecs, Toltecs—you name it."

"And was I to understand from James that you can actually read Mayan hieroglyphs?"

"Yeah, for the most part. They're not actually hieroglyphs like the Egyptians used. They're more like logoglyphs like in Japanese or Chinese. They usually represent a morpheme—a word or concept, while Egyptian glyphs stood for syllables, which is more like the way our alphabet works," he explained as he entered his study. "Well you heard me in the front talking to them," he shouted across the room, but no one stood there. "Don't be so surprised. I told you James and Tim were coming!" He paused as the other three men looked at each other in puzzlement. "He's their friend—er—colleague. You know." He stopped again as if to listen to the office chair speak back to him. James just shot the other two men a look that asked them to say anything. "Okay, okay," Matt sighed. "But get ready, I'm going to sit on you." He sat and turned to the men. "Let's see it. What have you got?"

James set the box down on the cluttered desk and opened it once again to reveal the cloth wrappings inside. He slipped his fingers underneath and lifted the weighty bundle, and finally unwrapped it for Matt to take hold of the precision-carved jaguar. Matt's eyes widened and his lips curved with exuberance as he ran his fingers over the details.

"This is exquisite," he gushed. "I've never seen such detail in a classic period piece like this. And so well-preserved. It's a Bahlam jaguar god. Probably represents the god of terrestrial fire and war, which is associated with day and night, the underworld, the afterlife, time, and of course . . . fire and war."

"Mayan?" Reed asked.

"Oh, for sure," Matt confirmed and then turned it over to study every inch. "As I said, this is probably classic period art, somewhere between two hundred and nine hundred AD."

"Where from?" James inquired.

"Oh, geez," Matt half laughed. "Who knows? This time period saw the rise of the really big-ass city-states, you know? Any one of which probably would have been home to this idol. There were so many. Calakmul. Uaxactun. Tikal. Palenque. Take your pick. But it's impossible to tell where from just the idol. Where did you get this?"

"Hidden in the concrete staircase at Maison Rouge," Tim said.

"Galveston?" Matt puzzled. "*That* Maison Rouge? Jean Lafitte's Maison Rouge?"

"The same," James confirmed.

"I just figured out where I recognized you from." Matt turned his head to a surprised Reed. "Shut up!" he yelled at the chair again. "You're on that BBC show. Um," he searched for the title in his head, "*What If . . .* I love that show. A celebrity in my house," he beamed. "Anyway, didn't you also mention some documents?"

"Yeah, here in the box." James retrieved the documents and handed them to his friend. "The Spanish captain's log says they got the jaguar during an expedition to somewhere called Noh Peten."

"Oh, well shit. I know right where that is." He turned and clicked on an icon on his desktop to bring up a global satellite map program. "Take a look," he said, and zoomed in on Central America. "See this big northern province of Guatemala? There's Belize to the east, and this huge province is Peten. This is Lake Peten Itza. This little island here in the southern area of the lake—that's Flores. But it was once the Mayan city of Nojpeten, or Noh Peten. It's also been called Tayasal."

"Holy shit. Do you see what's up here to the northeast?" James pointed to the screen.

"Ah yes," Matt smiled. "Tikal. The greatest Mayan capital of the classic period. The New York City of the Mayan world. That's probably where your jaguar came from."

"Tikal." James's head tilted back in thought. "Wow."

"Yeah, man, this is like, the center of the Mayan world, dude," Matt added. "It's where some scholars believe the famous long-count Mayan calendar was devised. It's like a vortex—hell, UFO researchers claim that this *is* some sort of interplanetary or cross-dimensional vortex. They have all kinds of videos of UFOs in the area and shit. Crazy stuff. Weird place."

"Can you read the glyphs?" Tim asked.

"Yeah," Matt said, and shook himself out of that rabbit hole of thought. "Yeah. Forgot. Let's see." He read at the bottom of the captain's log page. "Hmmm . . . It looks like it might be incomplete. It just cuts off."

"What does it say?" Reed asked with a touch of impatience.

"Um," he scanned the writing again. "Well, I can tell. It's in the Itza dialect—a late one. Weird."

"Why is that weird?" James asked.

"Well, the Itza are known to have been present in the area—even founded the city of Noh Peten, which is where your town of Flores is today. It was the last independent Mayan kingdom to submit to the Spanish. Oddly so. Cortes even visited this place in the fifteen twenties and no one ever burned it to the ground. They just willingly submitted to the Spanish one day."

"That *is* strange." Tim rubbed his chin. "Like they had something to hold over the Spanish; some kind of bargaining chip almost."

"But I'm more interested in why you think this is so strange that the Itza wrote the inscription on the stella," James said.

"The Itza are more associated with the Yucataan Maya. As you know, the Maya were loosely associated with one another by culture, ethnicity, and language, but they had their differences and controlled certain areas of Central America as city states often at war with one another. It's not unlike the city-states of ancient Greece—Sparta, Athens, Corinth, Thessaly, etc. Or like tribal groups in Africa. It's a mistake to assume all the Maya were the same and that they were all friends."

"I got you."

"Well, the Itza—as in the major city complex of Chichen Itza—were somehow driven out of the Yucatan by another group from further north out of what is now Tabasco. The Itza eventually settled in the Peten region of Guatemala, which is where Tikal is."

"So they're connected to Tikal," Tim stated.

"Kinda, not really. That's why it's weird. This Itza migration happened probably in the fourteenth century, long after Tikal had declined. The idea of this idol associated with this stella doesn't make sense. The idol would be associated with a major place of worship, not some fourteenth century Itza village."

"Maybe the Itza became the caretakers of the religious sites at Tikal—took on responsibility for what most Maya would still consider sacred sites," Reed said.

"Maybe. Who knows," Matt said. "But as for the inscription . . . the guy who drew this was no artist, but if it's what I think it is . . . here goes." He paused and then recited. "The chosen seeks to control his fate. He seeks his blessing from the realm of the gods . . ."

"And that's where it stops?" James asked.

"Yeah. Again, it seems like it should say more," Matt pondered. "It doesn't give a specific location. But this is an interesting clue."

The four men fell silent for a moment, each with a goal to make sense of the vague passage.

"Realm of the gods," James spoke. "Who knows? Looks like a celestial concept. The equivalent of Heaven or Olympus. It doesn't actually sound like a physical location."

"I'm more interested in this controlling-your-fate stuff," Tim said.

"Yeah, and why the Society is so balls-to-the-ball hardcore about getting this idol," James added.

"The Society?" Matt perked from his contemplation.

"We've been followed and attacked twice since we left Galveston," Tim responded. "We think they're members of something called the Society of the Lost Dominion."

"That makes perfect sense. Those guys—"

"Wait, you've heard of them?" James gaped.

"Yeah, for sure." Matt leaned back in his chair. "It was supposedly founded right after the American Revolution—a sort of we're-pissed-off-that-we-lost-the-American-colonies club for the well-to-do English. Of course George III would have been a founding member, as well as wealthy lords who had business interests across the Atlantic."

"And military leaders," Tim added. "Lockyer. Packenham. Lord Liverpool. Sir Isaac Brock."

"Sure," Matt confirmed. "Those guys have all been listed as members of the Society, though it officially doesn't exist, of course. It was their intention to get the colonies back and reverse the outcome of the revolution. When the British navy started boarding American ships and conscripting American sailors in the early days of the U.S., whose idea do you think that was? Who do you think was behind the War of 1812; the British invasion of the U.S.? And throughout the years, they've been tied to numerous activities in British territories that had gained their independence. They were involved with fighting the IRA in Ireland and Northern Ireland after the Easter Rebellion. Speculation that they had something to do with the assassinations of Mahatma, Indira, and Rajiv Gandhi in India. Involvement in the Holy Land after taking possession of the former Ottoman Empire at the end of World War I. The assassination of Anwar Sadat in Egypt. Even the Lincoln assassination has been tied back to the Society."

"And so the meeting between Lockyer and Lafitte," James thought aloud. "Why did this happen? Is the idol really something of that much monetary value?"

"I wouldn't think so." Matt shrugged. "It's cool. It's well-preserved. It might be interesting to an art collector, but other than that . . ."

"The kind of deal they wanted to cut with Lafitte and the amount of trouble and danger Lockyer went through to even seek an audience in Barataria shouldn't have been worth the value of a piece of Mayan art," James pondered. "It doesn't make sense. What makes this thing so special?"

"The Mayans would have considered the idol supernatural," Reed said. "And the glyphs from the stela speak of changing one's fate by divine power."

"Of course," Tim agreed. "But they were superstitious pre-Columbian Mayans. It doesn't have real powers."

"But maybe the Society thinks it does," Matt said. "Think about it. Rational, modern people all over Europe and America believe symbols and objects like crucifixes and relics have special powers. Is it that hard to believe that the Society's members think this idol does too?"

"Maybe the Society thinks they can change the fate of the British Empire," James said. "Maybe they think it can—I don't know—change history?"

"Which is why it was such a priority in eighteen fourteen—they were losing this war," Tim noted. "This was their last desperate attempt."

"That's ridiculous, though," James sneered. "A magic idol?"

"We got shot at, James," Tim reminded him. "It doesn't matter if it's magical or not. Someone thinks it is. And they have guns. So we need to figure out what to do. Do we hand it over? I mean, it's just a piece of limestone, right? Who gives a shit? Get them off our backs."

"Good point," Reed agreed.

"I just can't shake this feeling." James stared into the computer screen and the satellite image of the Guatemalan jungle. "Laffite went to great lengths to hide and protect it. Something tells me that would be a bad idea."

Chapter 14

With a robotic slide, the double doors parted, and out into the humid chill stepped James Beauregard. He moved with a pace between brisk and casual, his hands protected from the night air within the warmth of his jean pockets. His head remained hung with a view mainly of the badly weathered asphalt of the hotel parking lot, yet caution told him he might do well to pay closer attention to his surroundings.

He arrived at the small side street off from the main drag, which was not busy, but a lifetime of looking both ways held him planted in the strip of St. Augustine grass between the sidewalk and the road. He burst into a trot to cross, even with no traffic, to reach the brightly lit filling station on the other side. Nestled into the dark recesses of the lot next to a twenty-four-hour diner, the heavier side of Nineties rock crept into the night, muffled by a heavy, metal door.

James took hold of the simple, rusted steel handle and pulled to unleash the full force of the gritty crunch of the guitar that blared from the speakers behind the bar. In an instant, a wall of smoke and beer-stained air welcomed him into the shadowy black-and-wood-grain atmosphere where coeds mingled with the area's off-the-clock service industry workers with inebriation almost certain in their futures.

He spotted his party at the bar, an empty stool between them saved for him to belly up. Already, a bourbon awaited, its ice melted and a moat of condensation in a circle around it, but cold and refreshing enough to do the trick. He sat and swigged as the other two men acknowledged his arrival with an initial nod.

"All checked in, I presume?" Reed lifted and sipped his scotch.

"We're good," James mumbled over the cigarette in his lips as he lit. "It'll be a nice temporary place to rest for the night, and tomorrow we'll figure out where to go from here."

"What a fucking day," Tim sighed. Everyone gestured agreement. "Talk to Noelle?"

"Yeah, she's fine. Asking too many questions and I just don't feel like answering all of them. Plus, she obsesses, so I don't want to freak her out with the whole getting shot at thing."

"You guys doing okay?" Tim detected a tone in James's voice that differed from what he saw in previous interactions with Noelle.

James stared into his bourbon like an oracle. He watched the droplets of water roll down the side of the glass and into the pool accumulated on the varnished bar. He contorted his lips as his senses were filtered down to only the sight of his drink and his thoughts about Noelle.

"I love her," he said, but nothing more.

"But . . ." Tim raised a brow.

"But," James stopped for a moment. "I'm not sure I want to marry her."

"But if you love her . . ." Tim protested. "You proposed, dude."

"It's not really her. It's . . ." he paused. "It's Abigail and Max."

"Who are they?" Reed asked.

"Who *were* they?" James said. "My wife and son. They," he choked on his words, "died some years back. Drunk driver."

"So you feel as though you're cheating on your late wife. Betraying your family," Reed continued his inquiry.

"God . . ." James buried his face in his palm. "I'd give anything to have them back. Anything."

"Does that include giving up what you have with Noelle?" Reed asked.

"Yeah—I mean; I love her but—I don't know. I don't know how to feel. How I'm *supposed* to feel. Marriage? She already lives with me, and that's hard enough sometimes. I keep waiting for Abigail to turn the corner and see me. I don't want to hurt Noelle, but Jesus."

"This is perfectly normal. It will pass. You'll get through it," Reed reassured, and patted him on the back.

"Yeah, man. Everything's going to be fine," Tim burst in his classic forwardness. "Come on, Noelle's fuckin' hot! What's not to love? Put your past behind you, bro!"

Images flooded James's head—images of his late wife in all her glory. Her dirty-blond curls and bright, love-filled eyes already open when he woke from a good night's sleep. Her perfect pink lips mouthed "Good morning" with a pillowy softness. Then another image was conjured. He remembered turning the corner to see Tim, his best friend, with his hands all over her at the table. He could feel his heart rate increase and his temperature rise. He recalled the discomfort and hurt in her eyes as she caught sight of her husband. His muscles tightened and trembled as a fist in all its white-knuckled rage became airborne and flew to the left to find its place across Tim's jaw. A glass arced across the smoke-filled air, followed by ice and an amber brown rain of spirits as Tim tipped out of his stool and lay reeling on the dingy concrete floor.

The music raged on, but most conversation in the room stopped as onlookers broadened the perimeter around the center of commotion. Tim rolled over and clutched his jaw for a few moments, dazed and stunned on the floor while James stood over him as Achilles over the fallen corpse of the mighty Hector. His breath was deep and labored, his fists clenched and ready for more battle as he stared down as his prey with impunity.

Tim was slow to stand. He smiled as he rose to his feet, a chuckle in the back of his throat. In an instant, as if a switch were flipped, the casual recovery became a ravenous attack. Tim dropped his shoulder and buried it deep into James's torso to drive the man across the bar. They crashed into the console of an arcade golf game, causing its plastic construction to falter and break under the stress. Tim lifted his stance and threw a right, which found its target on James's chin. He recovered quickly to throw a reciprocal punch and then wrap up his opponent and wrestle him to the ground in a struggle for leverage against one another.

A giant of a man pried Tim to one side as the bartender, who had hopped the bar like a gazelle, took hold of both of James's arms. The two were separated and dragged through the door and into the street. Reed, slow and slightly impaired, followed in a gangly stroll, his drink still in hand. He stepped into the night air as the bartender plucked the drink from his grip.

"Take this shit somewhere else or I'm calling the cops," the bartender warned as he and the bouncer reentered the bar.

The door shut and the music again was muffled. The party inside resumed as the three of them were soon forgotten. Tim and James each parked their posteriors upon the concrete curb outside the bar. Heads hung low and throbbed almost to the beat of the rock and roll that droned from inside. Reed stood over them with not a word uttered and watched the two rub their jaws and lick their wounds.

"Let me guess," Tim spoke up. "You've been waiting for a long time to do that."

"Years."

"Was it everything you dreamed it would be?"

"I'm not disappointed," James said.

"Yeah, well you hit like a bitch."

James chuckled. He lifted his head and smiled over at Tim. He put his arm around him, and pulled him in. "I love you, bro."

"Love you too."

"I'll never understand you Americans." Reed sighed and shook his head.

"We square?" Tim asked.

"Square," James replied. "Let's get to the hotel and get some shut-eye."

Chapter 15

Yellowed fangs flashed from beneath whiskers as the fierce jungle cat roared and snarled in warning. He stood, circled, and approached as if to make that final move and end the life of his prey. But instead, he changed his demeanor. He tamed; no more threat. He turned to walk away into the dense foliage, but then stopped to turn and look back. His eyes invited. As he again walked toward the jungle, a strange sound filled the air, distant at first. It increased in intensity and amplitude until it was more imposing, then deafening in this environment.

James's eyes opened to darkness. A single shred of light pierced the black through a barely parted gap between the two curtains across the room. On the nightstand, his cell phone lit and chimed its outdated electronic tune. A few moments went by as his breathing hastened and his heart rate increased. The phone ceased to be a blur, and James sat up in the bed. He rubbed his bruised chin with a wince and then leaned over to read the display on the phone's screen.

Matt Davidson?

"Do you know what time it is?" James said in a dull tone as he made his way for the bathroom. He felt around for a light switch on the smooth, cold tiles on the wall and flipped it on with a shock to his narrowing pupils. He closed the door, dropped his shorts, and sat to urinate as he listened for Matt's response.

"Yeah, like mid-morning," Matt chuckled. "What did you guys do last night?"

"Long story," James grimaced. "What's up?"

"Are you peeing? Are you peeing while you're on the phone with me?"

"Yes." James's tone became impatient. "And I'm probably not going to stop at that. So I'd spit it out."

"Dr. Reed," he snickered. "I remember why he seemed familiar."

"Yes, from his show on BBC," James sighed. "I thought we established that."

"No, I know. I mean," Matt stumbled, paused, and started again. "Yes, I do recognize him from that, but there was something else. I couldn't put my finger on it. But I did some research, and there it was. I knew I had seen his name and face somewhere else."

"What are you talking about?"

"Rylan Reed was not born Rylan Reed," Matt explained with a heightened tone of enthusiasm. "He was born Rylan Morehouse Lockyer-Reed."

"Lockyer?"

"Yes. His mother, member of the aristocratic Lockyer family, married Colonel Stratton Reed of the Royal Air Force in nineteen forty, just prior to the Battle of Britain. Rylan was born late the next year while Stratton was away at war and unable to give any input for naming the baby. The Lockyer family was insistent upon the hyphenate so that the Lockyer name would be represented."

"Oh shit. Rylan Reed is descended from—"

"Captain Nicholas Lockyer," Matt finished the sentence. "According to my sources online, Dr. Rylan Reed, as he goes by now, is linked directly with the Society of the Lost Dominion. It's even thought that he might be the current chancellor of the group, inheriting the position from his maternal grandfather when he died."

James had already stood and pulled up his boxer briefs. He stumbled from the bathroom into the dark, cold hotel room. *Why can't the light switches ever be easy to find in these places?* He rushed through the room in frustration, drawn to the window by the beacon sliver of light. He stood there blasted by the cold air from the air conditioning unit and ripped open the curtains to flood the room with sunshine. He turned to see Tim toss in the bed furthest away and groan in disapproval. But the other bed was empty. James's stomach tightened as he scanned the room for Reed's belongings, only to find that they were gone.

"Jesus Christ," he uttered. He paced, turned, and paced the other way with the feeling that he should do something, yet unsure what that might be.

"What?" Tim jumped up and rubbed his eyes. "What? What?"

"Reed's gone," James yelled, and then ran over to his own suitcase. He rifled through it, clothes and toiletries tossed in every direction. "The jaguar. It's gone." He stood with a sick look on his face. "That's it. He ripped us off."

"Why?" Tim asked, still groggy.

"He might be the chancellor of the Society of the Lost Dominion," James explained.

"And those guys who were chasing us?" Tim stood, more alert. He thought for a moment. "I thought I saw the guy hesitate when he drew the gun on Reed in the gas station. I remember thinking that was odd. But I shrugged it off."

"Reed has a son," Matt said, "who is also linked to the Society. Nicholas Lockyer Reed. I'm texting you his picture now."

A few seconds passed and James's phone chimed. He pulled the phone away and opened the text. "It's him." He looked at the photo and recognized one of the men from the day before. "Same guy. It's his fucking son." He turned the phone and showed Tim. "Thanks, Matt," he said, again placing the phone to his ear. "Hey man. I've got to go. Someone's beeping in." He looked at the screen. "Oh, it's the old lady. Gotta go, man." He pressed the SEND button to switch lines. "Hey babe."

"I know we've grown close, but pet names already? It may take a few more dates and a little more scotch," a deep British voice said on the other end.

"Reed," James growled. "Why do you have—Oh Jesus."

"You're a very smart man," Reed crooned. "Very smart, indeed, but let's see how smart you are."

"If you—"

"Watch yourself, Dr. Beauregard. You're not being smart. Now listen closely. Noelle is coming with us."

"I want to know she's okay," James said calmly but with hate in his voice. "Prove it to me."

A few moments passed. Tears accumulated along the edges of his eyes as he trembled and fidgeted his feet.

"James," a small, distant voice called. "James."

"There you are," Reed interrupted. "Now listen closely. She's coming with us. When we have what we want, we will send her home. That is a promise."

"You're not exactly the greatest example of trustworthy right now," James said. "How do I know you're not going to—"

"Kill her?" Reed laughed. "We are not monsters, James. We are not psychopaths. We have as deep a respect for human life as anyone else. We will not kill her just because we feel like it. But make no mistake. We have been looking for this for a *very* long time, and now that we have the jaguar—now that we are so close to what we lost—we will stop at nothing. If you try to follow, we do what we must."

"I swear to God," his fears converted to rage as his voice roared. But he stopped. There was a faint click and then an electronic tone to indicate the call was over. "Shit." He looked up at his friend. "They've got her. They're taking her."

"To Guatemala?"

James did not answer. He thought on that for a moment. *Noh Peten. Guatemala. Tikal.* Several moments passed as he chewed on his fingernail. He paced back and forth, deep in his own thoughts.

"What now, Jim?" Tim trembled as he spoke. "Police? FBI? Notify the State Department? The embassy there? Interpol? Shit, what?"

"What the hell are they going to do?" He finally stopped pacing. "Nobody's going to believe that some secret society we learned about on a conspiracy theorist website kidnapped my fiancée and ran off to Mayan country to change the course of history. And even if they did, I don't see anyone rushing off to hike the remote jungles of Central America."

"So what? Take him at his word? We know who they are. He knows it. These people were instrumental in assassinations. They did everything they could to reclaim, expand, and preserve the British Empire. The Boer War in South Africa. Involvement in Afghanistan and Iraq. They stop at nothing to get what they want. You think they're going to just leave witnesses to their existence and their actions?"

"You're right," James stopped. "Yeah."

"So?"

"We have to go after her."

Chapter 16

Tim tapped his fingers on the steering wheel. He gripped and pulled at it as every muscle tensed in his arms. His head shifted from side to side with keen eyes under low brows. He scanned through every window. His leg bounced up and down like a piston within an engine block.

Weeds towered high above the cracked, crumbled concrete they sprouted from. Gang graffiti tarnished the dirty, painted bricks of the convenience store. The bass thundered from some passing vehicle as he eyed a group of young men as they strode up to enter the building. His grip tightened on the wheel as his heart rate briefly spiked. An old man with gray in his dark, scraggly beard and a tattered hood over his head exited the store and sat on the corner with a giant can of beer, still cold and dripping with condensation. Moments passed like hours as Tim watched the young men exit and slowly pass his car. Their eyes locked with his, but they kept moving and piled into a car across the lot. A sudden jolt of bass blasted with a vibration of some of the looser parts of the car. Then he came out. Tim finally exhaled, as if he had held his breath the whole time, and James opened the car door, then jumped in with his bag.

"Christ, it took you long enough." Tim did not wait for James to click his seatbelt before he shifted into reverse and backed out.

"You nervous?" James said with a grin.

"North of I-10, dude. North Baton Rouge. I was hoping for the best case scenario when those guys over there jump me into the gang."

"It's not that bad."

"You're right. Most of the murders on the Baton Rouge nightly news come out of the ritzy areas, right? Look around. We're in the land of gangs, liquor stores, and bail bond shops. We're in the ghet-to," he chuckled. "Speaking of liquor. You get what you need?"

James pulled back the brown paper bag a bit to reveal a big black label and a full fifth of brown Tennessee grain alcohol. A smile formed on his face. With everything on his mind, he was at ease. His hands clung to the bottle. Its weight provided comfort. It was full; waiting. It invited.

The shiny rental car sped up the weathered boulevard. St. Augustine grass, thick, overgrown, and dotted with white clover, carpeted the sides of the streets, damp with morning dew. A diorama of fast-food joints, thrift stores, and decayed homes passed as they skirted the chain-linked perimeter of the airport, and then took a left down a driveway on the south side. A series of metal buildings, hangars, and the control tower grew larger in their approach. They parked outside a hangar labeled with a huge sign that read "A1 Aviation." No time was wasted as they hopped out, then walked up to a heavy metal door they promptly flung open.

"Hello?" James's voice echoed within the spacious metal hangar.

A few workers went about their jobs on the far side, all in orbit of the sleek white Gulfstream being prepared for flight. Hoses attached to the wing fueled the craft while people scurried up and down the steps with boxes of supplies.

"This can't be cheap," Tim said as he watched all the people involved work to prepare for this flight.

"It's not," James said. "We just called them an hour ago, and look at them."

"And almost ready," a very non-Baton Rouge dialect sounded from behind them. "Scott Rucker," a man said as he strutted up from out of the office. He extended his hand and flashed his perfect white teeth. He had the look and style of a Banana Republic model who had spent too much time in the tanning beds.

"James." He took the man's over-gripping hand. "And this is Tim. Almost done, you said?"

"Yeah, just a little more fuel. And some of the comforts you're going to want. We'll be ready shortly. The captain's just finishing up the flight plan. You guys want to wait over here for a few while we finish loading up?"

They followed him to a bench that looked out of place in this environment. It was a classic park bench set not in the greenery of a park, but against the industrial concrete and metal of an airport hangar. The two men sat as Scott walked off to oversee the preparation of the charter jet. James leered at the craft as sweat began to form on his stubbled lip. The hair on the sides of his head dampened as his body shook. His breaths grew shallow as his heart and stomach fluttered and skin crawled with all the feeling of the inside of an insectarium. He reached into his pocket to retrieve his pack of smokes. He lifted a cigarette to his mouth and stuffed the orange filter between his lips as he flicked frantically to get it lit. Finally, a puff filled his mouth, and then his lungs. With an exhale, his nerves calmed, but then were up again. He reached into his bag, and with haste, ripped the cap off his bottle of whiskey. He proceeded to guzzle giant gulps that flamed down his esophagus into his waiting belly. *Ah, better.*

"Not a fan of flying, are you?" Tim glanced at his friend, but he did not respond. "That's new."

"That's old."

"Old to you. New to me. We've been out of touch in recent years, remember? When did that start?"

"I don't know. A while back."

"Okay, guys, you ready to board?" Scott called out across the hangar.

"After . . ." Tim hesitated as the two of them stood and moved toward the plane. "After the accident? Max and Abigail?"

"I don't know. Maybe. Yes."

"Have a nice flight," Scott beamed like a car salesman to no response. He simply eyed James shakily climb the stairs with his lips permanently attached to a bottle of whiskey.

They climbed into the soothing beige interior with plush leather seats and plenty of space. Pristine carpets ran the length of the fuselage, trimmed by lightly-stained wood runners and track lighting.

"Nice." Tim grinned as he took his seat. "I've got to travel with you more often."

In the same moment, James hastily sat, grabbed a paper bag from one of the seats, and vomited into it with the most horrid of liquidy roars any man could make. The sudden stench of stomach acid and whiskey filled the confined space as a sour look crossed Tim's face.

"Jesus, you must really love her." Tim grimaced, upon the brink of nausea himself. "And I take back what I said about traveling with you more often."

James handed the bag to a horrified flight attendant who gripped it with the ends of only one finger and a thumb, and hauled it away. He nodded silently to his friend. A moment passed as Tim thought, staring at his phobia-stricken partner.

"Don't forget about what's important," he said, and patted James's knee with firm masculinity. And then the jet taxied out of the hangar and into the South Louisiana sun.

Chapter 17

Fluffy white tufts moved along the azure currents as small flower petals down a stream. So beautiful, but so mundane, they drifted by in an endless parade of small clouds above the warm, tropical gulf waters, all framed by a small double-paned window. The hum of the engines lulled Noelle in her tan leather seat. She barely blinked, her head unmoved, propped upon her hand and her legs tucked beneath her.

"You should eat," Dr. Reed interrupted the white noise as he gestured toward the plate of eggs, bacon, and raisin toast set upon the polished wood grain table before her. "What's the point of flying in a private jet if you can't enjoy the perks?" he said, but to no response. He waited a moment. "You would not speak to us, so we had to guess your tastes based on your deep-south upbringing. Perhaps something more aristocratic— eggs benedict, perhaps." He sipped his Earl Grey. "Tea? Coffee?"

"I'd like a big, steaming cup of coffee," she finally spoke.

"Ah, she speaks. Maybe we could—"

"So I can throw it in your face."

"On second thought . . ." He soured as Nick and Rupert giggled, their faces stuffed with breakfast morsels.

The silence resumed. She sunk again into the passing of clouds, water, and sky. The breakfast remained untouched and Reed enjoyed his tea, but kept his old gray-green eyes on the young woman. He allowed her those thoughts that filled her head. He was sure of what they were. Questions, no doubt, abounded. Insecurities? Fears?

"I've never been to Guatemala," he finally spoke, though Noelle remained transfixed on the scene beyond her window. He looked out his own, briefly. "I look forward to it. So different from back in England. Warmth. Humidity. Almost primal, gritty, earthy culture. Such history," he rambled, almost to himself, though he knew she could hear. "The level of civilization possessed in comparison to elsewhere in the Americas—in the world, even, in some cases. It's amazing. The expertise in building great pyramids and structures with such primitive technology. It defies everything logical in historical and archaeological study. We've been looking for this for a long time. One of the great vertices of the world."

The statement struck Noelle's consciousness in a way that she instantly turned her head. She peered at him through her tired, worried eyes, ready now to take in the old professor's rant.

"There are many, supposedly with different properties," he continued. "We searched them all. Controlled those territories over the centuries. India. China. Egypt. The Holy Land. The Indus River Valley—Pakistan now. The old land of Mesopotamia. All had advanced civilizations with great monuments beyond the scope of human capability. Advanced technology; systems of writing. They all studied the sky; devised calendars. We searched the British Empire over. We helped keep it; maintain it through war, political posturing, trade—whatever. Hitler had the same ideas, you know. That's why it was so imperative to defeat him. And, well, that whole Holocaust thing. But which was the right vortex? Each has its qualities—most of them still a mystery to us, really. But this one the Society always had a feeling about. The one that would give us the ability to preside over space and time. Reclaim our destiny. British destiny."

"What in the hell are you talking about?" She narrowed her eyes. "Vortex? What society? Are you bat-shit insane?"

"The Society," he chuckled and paused to regain composure. "The Society of the Lost Dominion. Formed soon after we lost the North American colonies," he explained. "The colonies were essential to the growth of the empire. His Majesty's Navy was its backbone, a legacy that stretched from the defeat of the Spanish Armada to the decimation of Napoleon's fleet. And the timber for all those ships had to come from somewhere."

"North America," she said.

"Can you imagine," he half laughed with a degree of irritation, "the prosperity of the British Empire had they held those North American colonies into modern day with all the resources and lands eventually controlled by the United States?"

"Yeah, fine. I get it. But that's in the past. Why hang on to that bitterness? There's nothing you can do about it now."

"When my ancestors helped found the Society, the intentions were very straightforward," he stated with a level of seriousness. "The conflict that became known as The War of 1812. Regain the colonies and all their resources. But already, there were rumors of strange occurrences in various areas of the world—even parts of our empire. Uncanny lights in the skies, for example. Strange occurrences near the sites of these old civilizations. It's amazing how similar they all are. Hieroglyphic-style writing. Advanced geometry in their highly advanced structures and architecture. Similar gods and religious beliefs involving celestial creatures appearing from the heavens. It's carved into tablets, temples, and monuments all over these ancient lands. But then the Jaguar idol." He opened the box on the small table before him and removed the stone piece. "And the Spanish captain's log recovered in the Caribbean. They were clues that the place we were looking for was in the west—somewhere in the jungles of Mayan Central America. The place Juan Ponce de Leon himself had been looking for, mistakenly, in modern-day Florida."

"Christ," she giggled. "Are you crazy fucks looking for the Fountain of Youth? That's what this shit's about? That's why you kidnapped me? The goddamned Fountain of Youth?"

"Ponce de Leon looked for a fountain or waters of some sort; the Waters of Bimini some historians called it—again a mistake. In reality, it had nothing to do with waters, or even youth, exactly. It had to do with turning back time. An older man might, upon discovering a way to somehow rewrite history or change his destiny, go back and return to his youth. Another might set himself on a path that carries him to wealth and prosperity. But the Society of the Lost Dominion has a deeper purpose—a greater good."

"Changing history," she understood. "You want to change the outcome of the Revolutionary War."

"Not only regain what we lost, but assure that we never lost it." Fever filled his eyes. "And this jaguar is the key. This temple; this city of Tikal, somehow is the key. It has to be. It's a major vortex."

"An interdimensional wormhole of some sort to change history?" she scoffed. "That's the dumbest thing I've ever heard."

"It's the truth," he snapped, his voice curled with a snarl. "This is the culmination of centuries of searching. This is our time! Now!"

"Okay, fine, Gene Roddenberry," she snarked as she watched him calm, sit, and wipe his forehead with a handkerchief. "But what the hell do you need me for? Kidnap me away from my mother's before dawn? Drag me off to Central America? What good am I? If you need help finding this place or figuring out what you're supposed to do, shouldn't you have taken my fiancé? I'm just a geologist."

"I need you for insurance," he said. "We don't need his expertise. We have this well under control. What I don't need is your husband to be growing a set of warrior balls and crusading out here to get you."

"Let me guess. You told him if he tries, or goes to the cops, you'll kill me. You don't look like the killing sort."

"I'm not," he smiled. "But then again, we have waited a very long time for this moment, and absolutely nothing shall stand in our way. We will do what is necessary." He paused for a sip of his tea. "And I think James will do the smart thing. He does not appear to be the crusading sort. Too brainy."

"You don't know my fiancé very well," she smirked, their history in mind. "He'll come for me."

Reed leaned back and propped his right leg up on his left knee. He snickered, which became an amused laugh as he peered again out the small window to his left.

"What's so funny?"

"It appears it is you who doesn't know your fiancé very well." He turned again to her, a smile still wide on his face. "Why just last night, with a little help from his beloved bourbon, he confided in us some doubt."

"What do you mean *doubt*?" Her face lost a bit of its color.

"Doubt that he even wanted to marry you," he said with amusement. "Don't be so sure he's coming for you."

She grew quiet, and withdrew into herself. She sunk into her seat as far as it would allow. Her legs again tucked under and her softened eyes turned back to the window as she bit at her thumbnail and tried to hide her emotions.

Chapter 18

"Beautiful," Reed marveled. "Simply breathtaking. Like Venice in the heart of Central America." He gazed out the dingy window of the car as it cleared the little suburb of San Benito and began upon the manmade earthen causeway over the waters of Lago Peten.

He clutched the old box close in his lap. He even caressed it a little as he remained glued to the glass like a young child on his first road trip in the family station wagon. A casual, pleasant grin took permanent residence on his face. No one disturbed him.

A leather-faced, middle-aged man silently operated the car, Rupert discontent in the front seat next to him. He sulked, sunken into the stained seats with his arms crossed atop his bulged belly. A rounded, stubble-encrusted second chin protruded from beneath his dark, shorn beard as his eyes remained transfixed upon the weathered asphalt that approached ahead.

"Almost heavenly. Like entering some sort of Mesoamerican Olympus," Reed seemed to mutter to himself. "Lofty. Unattainable. Otherworldly. No wonder the Maya found it so sacred a place."

"And easy to defend," Nick added as he took in a lengthy view of Noelle's tanned legs to his left, something that tightened her crossed arms and caused her eyes to roll. "Probably one of the reasons why they held out against the Spanish for so long."

"Quite right." Reed glanced over at his son. "Quite right. Don't you think, my dear?" he nudged Noelle. "Don't you think this place is breathtaking?" But there still was no vocal response. He nodded. "Don't worry. This will all be over soon."

The car drew ever closer to the small island city. Stucco walls rose in the humid lake air, crowned by reddish-orange Spanish tiles. In the near distance, lush green hills peaked over those rooftops from across the lower arm of the lake.

"¿Dónde quieres ir?" The driver peeked into the back seat through the rearview mirror.

"Um," Reed uttered as he leaned forward toward him, a blank look apparent on his face. He swiveled his head to his son, who threw up his hands without a clue.

"¿Dónde quieres ir?" he repeated, and separated his hands briefly from the wheel with a growing of frustration.

"Um," Reed uttered again. "I . . ." He continued to look about the car for help for several moments.

"He wants to know where you want to go," Noelle scoffed.

"How do you know? Do you speak Spanish?" Rupert turned and faced the backseat with some labor.

"No, but 'dónde' is kind of a dead giveaway," she laughed at the men. "All these plans and all this destiny. Changing history," she chuckled some more, "and you idiots can't even get past a cab driver and a little simple Spanish."

"Fine." Nick nodded, and waited a moment, puzzled. "Where *are* we going? A temple of some sort? Some site?"

"Not here," Reed said. "Not on this island. This might have once been Noh Peten, but now it's a fairly new Spanish city. No temples. No plazas and ball-courts."

"But that's ultimately what we're looking for, right?" his son reasoned.

"Of course," Reed affirmed. "Indeed so. But first we must find this stela described here." He retrieved the Spanish captain's log from within the box. "These glyphs are incomplete. And they must be related to the jaguar if they were found and kept with it all these years. This writing came from a Mayan stela in this very city. We have to find it first and complete the message before we can possibly know what to do next," he explained, which drew a single chuckle and a sinister smirk from the woman beside him. "Yes?" He cocked his head.

"How long ago is that piece of paper from? You're assuming that stela is even still there. For all we know, it's long gone—in a museum half way around the word—and you're at a dead end."

A sour look graced his face as he took his eyes off of her and gazed out the window for a moment. His silence was an acknowledgement. He had not thought of that. He hoped the Guatemalan government treasured their past and preserved it. He then peered forward into the mirror to see the driver's eyes still imploring a destination or direction.

"We need to find the stela, but what good is finding it if we can't read it?" He regained composure.

"Is there anyone still around who could possibly read it?" Rupert asked.

"I just came from a man's house yesterday who read what is on this page," Reed confirmed. "It's reasonable to believe there are people here who can read ancient Itza text."

"Maybe a shaman of some sort?" Nick suggested. "Do those even still exist?"

"Yeah, I would think everyone here is pretty much Catholic, right?" Rupert agreed.

"Yes, but there are those who still perform Mayan rituals; who use sacred plants to treat illnesses and such amongst the locals," Reed explained. "We need a . . ." Dr. Reed spoke loud enough for the driver to hear, but paused to think of how to word it in a recognizable English format that the man might understand without knowledge of the language. "A shaman," he blurted but with no positive reaction from the driver. "Holy man. We need a holy man."

"Holy man," the driver repeated, clearly in thought. "Ah, padre," he smiled. "Padre."

"No, no, no," Dr. Reed quickly corrected. "No padre. We don't need a Catholic priest. We need a . . ." he paused again to think as he scanned the floor of the car as if to find an answer there. "A holy—shit—Mayan holy man. Mayan padre."

"Oh," the driver drew the word out longer. "Comprende. Sí. Ah Kin. Sí. Vamanos." He then stepped on the gas a little heavier to take them on into the city of Flores.

"Ah Kin?" Nick repeated. "You think that's right? Think he understands?"

"I have a feeling he does," Reed said.

The car rattled across the uneven pavement as it made the transition from the causeway to the tiny island city no bigger than a small suburban neighborhood. Distinctly non-European town natives in comfortable, simple cotton clothing designed for humidity crossed the combination of old cobblestones and modern asphalt as they went about their daily business. They were oblivious to these new foreign visitors and their intentions. The buildings were art—one- and two-story structures of stucco and wood with rickety galleries and exposed wiring that connected upward to the cables that descended from the lines above. Rusted signs labeled brightly-painted teal, orange, and even bright yellow homes and businesses that more resembled music, as if they were about to burst with a tropical drum beat, horns, and strings.

The car hugged ninety-degree curves, and at these comfortably high speeds, the driver moved his passengers with precision and familiarity about the city. It came to a rest, with a light squeal of rubber, and Dr. Reed opened his door. He stepped into the sweltering air in his beige suit worn casually and without a tie. He peered upward at the raspberry-pink two-story structure with wonder. The bright paint, in stark contrast with the dull earthen tones of most United States and European buildings, somehow forgave that the wood splintered and leaned in a way that might get it condemned elsewhere in the world.

"Dinero," the driver called out from the rolled-down window.

"Wait," he assured as he watched Nick drag Noelle out of the car by her arm. "We're coming back."

"Stay with the driver." Nick ducked his head to instruct Rupert. "Make sure he doesn't go anywhere. We're going to need him."

Reed looked back to the driver, imploring with his eyes. The driver pointed to one of three doors on the ground level of the home. As Nick approached from behind, Noelle forced along, Reed paused before the rustic entrance. He hesitated and tightened his posture before he knocked on the door. Several seconds passed without an answer or much of any sound before a crack appeared between it and the door jam. A small brown eye appeared between with a creak of the badly lubricated hinges.

"Sí?" she squeaked.

"Ah Kin?" Reed repeated the word the driver used in hope that it was correct.

The eye disappeared momentarily as her head turned. A mumble could be heard within. She answered the mumble with something in her own language that Reed could not understand. He fidgeted with his fingers and tapped his loafers, unsure if this was the right place. Then the door swung open to reveal a petite young woman with mysterious, dark, native features. She stepped aside and lowered her head to allow these aliens into the quaint home.

The hard, discolored gray walls were bare and cracked. Several pairs of bright, crisp eyes peered at them from their respective parts of the room. Two young boys sat upon the plain floorboards, their faces whitewashed in the light that shone from the old antenna-fitted television set. The matriarch stopped preparing food in the kitchen to the far recesses of the abode. A young man at the table stopped pulling the leaves from the stems of some tropical plant, yet the old man at the table, his skin dark and wrinkled, continued to prepare his sacred herbs as he made eye contact with Dr. Reed. It lasted for several moments as Reed watched the old man chew something unidentifiable with what was left of his teeth.

"Ah Kin?" Reed cocked his head and then took the slow nod of the old man as affirmation. "Ingles?" he inquired further, followed by another nod.

Reed slowly moved closer, each set of eyes set upon him as the floor creaked with age. He stopped just before the table, a polite grin still on his face. Nick hung at a distance, a watchful eye scanning the room at all times for any threat.

"I need a shaman. A Mayan priest who knows the language," Reed explained to the old man. "One who knows the religion and the land."

Several silent moments passed as the old man's look remained unchanged. His face bore understanding, as did his demeanor, and then he spoke.

"Why? What do you seek?"

"Ha!" Nick burst. "Like we'd tell you anything."

"Yes, we must," Reed disagreed.

"But we can't just—" Nick stopped as his father raised his hand to hush him.

"We must," he restated. "He must know what we seek, or he cannot help us." And then he presented the box.

Reed placed it upon the rustic table. Its weight produced a solid thud as it drew every interested eye in the room. The matriarch repositioned herself, as did the young woman while the two men at the table were drawn in as if by magnetic field. Reed lifted the lid and again removed the heavy, cloth-wrapped object. He slowly unwrapped it from its old off-white cloth and watched the mouth of the old man gape in wonder at an object that he had only heard of.

"Bahlam," the younger man gasped, and then peered at his elder in disbelief.

"Bahlam has led you here?" the old man spoke. "Has chosen you? Has chosen you to bring him home?" He grinned, somehow skeptical.

"Yes." Reed puffed out his chest a bit. "This has been our destiny for ages. And you will lead us to the stela. Is it still here? Here in town?"

"It is." The old man lowered his head and returned to his herbs. "It is here."

"Then we have to go." An added impatience was detected in Reed's voice. "Now. Lead me. Guide me."

The younger man's face turned a deeper color than the already reddish-brown hue. His eyes threatened to burst from their sockets as he slapped down on the table. "No! No!" he raged, and then began a rant in Spanish toward the old man across from him. Though Reed could not understand the exact message, he assumed it was of protest. "No," he turned to Reed. "Abuelito will not do this. Bahlam is a sacred treasure. He belongs to our people." He stood, aggression more apparent. "You will not use it for your advancement, and you will not take my grandfather."

He grabbed at the stone jaguar in an attempt to recover it from Reed, who held to it as tightly as an NFL running back. He struggled only for a few moments until Nick reached into his waistband and removed the sleek black pistol. He reached far across his body, almost around the other side of his own head, and then swiftly delivered a blow across the younger man's face that sent him to the floor unconscious and bleeding. Screams filled the room as the children tucked themselves into a far corner with their older sister and the matriarch stepped further back into the kitchen, all under threat from that hoisted firearm pointed at them. The old man did not move. He stared at the jaguar and then looked up at Reed as he put the artifact away.

"You will come with me." Reed guided the old man to his feet and led him toward the door as he pushed Noelle along the same path. "Stay here for a few minutes, Nick, while we go to the stela. Make sure these fine people don't alert the authorities." And they were out the door and into the cab once more.

Chapter 19

Echoed sounds of tropical birds chirped and bounced from each fat-trunked tree. They combined with other exotic accents of thick vines and bright flowers amid the lush greenery. Light beamed from small gaps in the canopy above in a shower of god-like solar essence that glowed in the wetness of air.

The cat's eyes remained fixed, almost devoid of emotion as he sat as a sentinel over the sacred jungle. He did not move. Rather, something else did—something nearby in the shadowy recesses of the dense foliage. The footsteps were unmistakable. Two feet stepped with grace upon the plants and fallen leaves. Then, a flash of some undiscernible white clothing, but it was brief. Whispers and dirty-blond hair appeared and vanished repeatedly with the occasional accompaniment of a gleeful child's laugh. The jaguar stood and slowly turned to enter the jungle as if to invite, but everything started to shake.

The first thing James could see when his eyes opened was the empty tan leather seat across from him. He gripped at anything he could in desperation—the armrest, his seat, and even the wall. His chest puffed out with every frantic breath, his eyes wide and terror-stricken as he tried to determine where he was. Dense forest passed in a blur beyond the small, circular windows as the plane rattled down the cracked, neglected runway and the pilot employed the flaps and brakes. His head jerked from side to side to take in his surroundings—the seats, the less-than-full bottle of whiskey on the table, his friend to his left.

"Welcome back," Tim chuckled from the seat across the aisle as he observed with an insensitive level of humor he took in the spectacle.

James gripped his armrests with white bloodless fingers as the jet slowed to taxiing speed. He closed his eyes tight and took hold of his own bodily functions. He took in a huge lungful of air and expelled it with control, repetitively slower than before until his fingers loosened and he opened his eyes. He rubbed them and leaned forward, and then glanced over at his amused partner. He reached across to the table and opened the bottle of amber goodness. It burned with delight in a fiery waterfall down his esophagus before it reached his belly with a glow. *Better*.

Soon, the craft had stopped and the pilot announced their arrival to beautiful San Benito, Guatemala. The attendant moved about the cabin stashing items and cleaning up others. The doors opened into the diminished orange daylight and the steps were lowered onto the tarmac. James and Tim extended their legs and stood with a back-arching stretch and popped vertebrae.

"Gentlemen," the captain crooned as he stepped out from the cockpit. "You're good to go."

"And you're just waiting here?" James still trembled.

"You have us until we get back to the States. Take as long as you need. But the meter is running."

"Hopefully we're not long." James shot a concerned look to his friend. "And hopefully we'll have a plus-one."

A heavy weight of doubt fluttered his heart and tensed his neck and shoulders as he exited the plane down the steps to the sun-fractured tarmac with his friend. His mind raced with worry with every step he took toward the dated regional airport and the ramp that led to it. The primal beauty of the rain forest-coated hills along the horizon could not distract him. He had spent the past few days with Dr. Reed, and had come to think that he knew him. He seemed to be a congenial old professor. Perhaps that was an indication that no harm would come to Noelle. But then, he had not expected the change of events, and that brought doubt. He had to get to her, and quick.

They entered the stale air of the small strip mall of an airport with brisk purpose in their step. The afternoon sun had begun its metamorphosis into one of evening. Time was an issue. Their eyes trained on the glass exit doors, they bypassed local vendors with special licenses to sell their hand-woven fabrics and replica Mayan trinkets. James continued to file behind Tim even as his eye caught a little Mayan jaguar figurine on a shelf at one of the vendors' stands.

As if by reflex, Tim's body jerked to the right as he extended his arm and snatched a small brochure from a wooden peacock-like stand of tourist information. He stopped to examine the mostly plain white advertisement and its fat red letter that spelled "FLORES" across the top.

"What is it?" James stopped to share in the observation.

"Dunno. Just caught my eye." He pointed to the color picture of a pristine off-white Romanesque cathedral. The two men studied the picture for a moment until Tim's eyes widened and he pointed to something in the bottom left corner of the photo. "Look. What's that look like to you?"

"A stela." James observed what appeared to be an ancient stone monument. "Look, you can *just* make it out. The glyphs. Think that's it?"

"If I were a bettin' man . . ."

They pushed forward through the doors and back into the moist air. James paused a moment, and looked down the curb until he found exactly what he was looking for. He spotted a short, round man who leaned against his grimy, badly-aged yellow cab. He had just folded the paper he was reading with the knowledge that another couple of flights had come in. It was time to sell. It was time to make some money.

"Hola," the cab driver echoed across the breezeway. "I take you. Where you go? San Benito? Ponderosa? Tikal?"

"Here." Tim pointed to the picture as they approached and then slowed.

"Ah, sí. Catedral de Flores." The cabbie grinned, and then placed his hat again upon his balding head. "Vamanos. Get in." He motioned them over as he rounded the car to get into the driver's seat.

The two Americans hesitated a moment. Each looked to the other, as if for permission, and then they both climbed into the oddly-scented backseat of the dated piece of transportation. Soon the car was wide open on the highways of north central Guatemala. San Benito materialized around them as the driver hurled the car along at harrowing speeds. No resorts could be seen. It was unlike what the average tourist sees in somewhere like Cozumel. There were no giant pools and cabanas. There were no Starbucks, chain eateries, or umbrella drinks. Only simple, plain buildings and homes. People went about their business, unmolested by consumerism that might otherwise have encroached from North America.

"God, I hope we're right." James leaned forward and buried his face in his hands.

"About what?"

"Flores. If we're in the right place."

"That's what it said in the captain's log," Tim reassured. "It said Flores. Not only are we in Flores, Guatemala, as the log describes, but we're near *the* Mayan capital of the classical period."

"I just worry."

"I know you do," Tim snickered. "It's what you do."

"I mean, what if two hundred years ago, there was another Flores somewhere and now the town has a different name. Or what if this captain fucked up somehow? Simple human error."

"Calm down."

"Or what if the stelae are no longer there—hauled away by some crazy reformist mayor of Flores in the Eighties in an attempt to modernize the town's culture or something," he panicked.

"Calm. Down." Tim placed a firm hand on his shoulder. "Besides, even if we're in the wrong place, Reed is too. And that means Noelle is here. That's all that matters."

James watched through the left rear window as the sun raced for the western horizon and glimmered the small pitched waves of Lago Peten with flecks of golden orange. They roared across the manmade causeway and under the welcome arch. The car screeched around the nearly ninety-degree curve that led into the island town. He made barely a touch of the brake and then navigated the little streets without pause to send townspeople to scurry aside in terror.

Within a few minutes, they had reached the center of the island. The streets became inclined as the car climbed for the summit of the island. The men could see, as the car slowed to round the central public square, the boxy taupe cathedral as it faced west and bathed in the evening glow.

"Parque Central," the cabbie announced as they finally stopped in front of the mission-like church.

"Looks like the Alamo," Tim observed as he stepped out.

"Or St. Louis Cathedral back home. But smaller. Definitely newer," he said as he reached into his walled and removed a twenty to hand to the man. He was sure he overpaid, but his attention was elsewhere.

"Gracias." The man took the money from his hand and left.

"Wait!" James reached out, but the man was already gone. "Shit. We're going to need a ride to Tikal. Damn it! You see any other cabs?"

"Nope. It's dead around here," Tim scanned. "Let's just find the stela."

"Damn." James continued to look for another cab, even in futility. "Okay, let me see the brochure." He and Tim squinted in the dying light. "Okay, there's the church, so the stela—there it is." He looked up from the brochure and pointed across the small park to a weathered stone monument sheltered by a wood-and-thatch Mayan-style hut.

They started across the concrete walkways of the well-kept park in the direction of the cathedral as it stood in the backdrop. But in between, nestled within an enclosure of pluming green palms, a raised orange and green pavilion stood within a circle of street lights that had already flickered on. To the side, the stela stood as a reminder of the town and the people's rich history. The two men could feel that emanate from the piece as they approached. A smile formed on both their faces, perhaps in awe of such a thing. Maybe it was just the sense that they had encountered something new, or more likely the idea that they were one step closer to finding Noelle.

Something caught James's eye beyond the stela, and as Tim stopped almost giddily, his counterpart moved a little beyond it. Tim puzzled as he stared blankly at his friend, and then peered out to see what James saw somewhat illuminated by the street lamps.

"Is that another stela?" Tim spewed. James moved for it, and after a brief pause to study the first monument further, Tim moved to the second as well. "And it's different than the other. Different image. Different glyphs."

"Shit." James looked around the perimeter of the pavilion. "Three, four, five of these things. And probably all different."

"Well," Tim started as he rubbed his chin, "how are we supposed to know which one it is without the page from the captain's log? Reed took that with the jaguar."

"I don't know." James paced in frustration. "I don't know. Fuck! I don't know."

"Hey," Tim beamed with a ray of hope. "We don't really need to know which one, right? We know where we're going—which site; which city. We know we're going to Tikal. If that's where they're going, we still know they have Noelle there and we can get her back," he explained, but could already see James shaking his head.

"We still need to know *where*, exactly," James lamented. "Tikal is a huge site with multiple complexes, courts, buildings, and temples. Without knowing specifically where to go, we stand less of a chance of catching them."

Despair clouded their presence. Their thoughts turned as dark as the countryside itself. They would have to go blindly and take their chances. They could not help but look around at the several stelae with a small glimmer of hope that they might remember the glyphs from the page, but it was useless, and they each knew it.

And then pink—bright pink—moved on the other side of the pavilion. Tim noticed immediately and inched that way to James's initial bewilderment. He turned his head enough to try to determine where he was going, and then he grinned. *Leave it to horn-dog here to spot a female in a pink tank top.* James followed, almost irritated. *Thinking with his penis at a time like this.* But as he drew closer, the mystique of the young woman captivated him somehow, as well. Magnitude in her silence changed the energy and awe abounded.

Tim approached as far as he could, and then stopped before he realized it was not himself that was the object of her attention. Her eyes were on James. She invited him closer as he drew near and passed his friend. He stopped with not a word, and waited.

"This is what you seek," she said, and patted the top of the short monolith with sweetness in her eyes. James stared into those eyes, drawn in as if they were quicksand. He shook his head with subtlety.

"How do you know . . . ?" James began in a stupor. "How do you know what we seek?"

"Hmm." she smiled but delayed for several long moments. "You are the one. He chose you."

"Chose," he stopped as his speech trailed off into softness.

"Chose you to return him," she gently asserted. "He belongs there with the rest. The rest of his kind. His kin."

"Who? What kin?"

"Bahlam, of course," she half laughed, his reaction silly to her. "The jaguar must return home and you must take him there. Only you. Not the other man. And you will be rewarded."

"Wait." He awoke from his trance. "What man? Was it an older man?"

"Sí. A bad man. He has Bahlam. He has mi abuelo."

"Did they have a woman with them? A young woman?" The words almost tumbled out of his mouth as he could not get them out quick enough.

"Sí. Please, you must find them. You must return Bahlam."

"I don't give a shit about Bahlam," James belted, wide-eyed. "I don't need a reward. I just want her back. Tell me how to find them."

"You have no choice," she told him with a smile. "You will return him, and you will have everything you seek. Everything you dream of."

"How do I find them?" he asked again, with extra effort toward calmness. "Can you read this?" He motioned toward the stela. "Can you tell us where to go; what to do when we get to Tikal?"

"Sí," she affirmed. "Mi abuelo teaches me. He is Ah-Kin. He is a medicine man. That is why they took him." She paused to study the stela for a moment, and then interpreted. "The chosen seeks to control his fate. He seeks his blessing from the realm of the gods on high where Bahlam resides. When the sun wakes on the day of equal light and dark, the chosen communes with him and will receive his blessing."

The two men stared at the glyphs with squinted eyes that promised to squeeze every last drop of knowledge and reason from their professors' brains. The girl fell silent, her message relayed. She allowed them time to think, patient and calm.

"Realm of the gods on high," Tim repeated. "On high. Realm of the gods sounds like a temple."

"We know we're going to Tikal," James said. "There are tons of temples. Actually very famous ones." He stopped for a moment as his eyes widened by double. "Shit, why didn't I think of this before. *The* temple to see at Tikal—the most famous one—is the Temple of the Jaguar. It's a damned pyramid."

"Realm of the gods on high," Tim concurred. "So we have to return the jaguar to the Temple of the Jaguar. And we are supposed to do it when the sun wakes—morning or dawn—on the day when day and night are equal. The equinox?"

"A day of great celebration," the girl spoke up. "Tomorrow is one of those days. There will be a celebration at Tikal and every temple in the Mayan land."

"The damned vernal equinox is tomorrow—the first day of spring," James spoke up. "A holy day to the Mayans. They often built their temples according to the sunlight cast and shadows produced by the rising and setting sun on the days of the equinoxes and solstices," he said.

"That's a lot of planning and only four days out of the year to get it right," Tim marveled.

"For sure. But they did it, and in lots of different sites. Get your phone out and pull up a map." James watched Tim remove the phone from his pocket and tap to start the program. He handed it off as James took to the navigation and zoomed it in on their location. "Look here.

This is the temple. The entrance faces due east while the back of it faces exactly west. It's perfect."

"And elevated precisely to be level with the horizon," Tim stated.

"Especially at dawn on the day of an equinox or a solstice," James almost chuckled. "We know exactly where they're going and when they're going to be here.

"Yeah, we just have to get there by dawn, or really long before." Tim began to look around. "And I don't see any cabs. Are we just going to have to walk it or something?"

"We have a car," the young lady said. "It isn't much, but you may take it if it will help."

"Yes. Thank you. Show us," James said to her, and she led them off into the shadows.

Chapter 20

Knuckles turned white with tighter grips of the armrests and tattered seat cushions as the little early-Nineties Japanese coupe gobbled up miles of aged blacktop with insatiable greed. Every bump or rough spot rattled the panels and threatened to remove the wheels. The moon ascended and allowed its reflective power to illuminate the subsistence fields, humble country dwellings, and crude fences. They flashed by in a blue-gray blur as gradually, farms gave way to more and more undisturbed forest, thick and virgin.

"It really was no trouble," James grunted as he braced himself against the passenger-side dashboard. "I could have driven."

"No one drives this car but me." The young lady smiled, her foot heavy on the accelerator. "No one else in my family drives at all."

Just as the foliage had thickened, the ceiba trees and other hardwoods cleared momentarily and a small welcome center appeared—thatch-roofed stores and souvenir shops built in a local, rural fashion. Bathed in the light of the approaching headlights, a faded yellow gateway of probably concrete and stucco towered ahead. Dark corrosion and weathering marks extended down the paint from the top. They blazed down the highway that led beneath the distinctive, nearly triangular Mayan archway and into the blackness of the Guatemalan jungle.

"We're here?" Tim asked from the back as he read the sign that welcomed visitors to Tikal National Park.

"No. That was just the entrance to the park. It is much bigger than just the temples."

"How much longer?"

"Maybe," she seemed to guess as she shrugged, "another ten miles?"

"We never got your name," James said as he watched the wall of night pass by.

"You never asked," she said sweetly. "You are that trusting? Get in a car with a stranger and ride off into the jungle?"

"You seemed legit," James said.

"What does that mean?" she puzzled.

"Never mind," he chuckled.

"Marta. My name is Marta."

"You seem to know a lot about the Maya, Marta," he said. "About the culture. Religion. Language?"

"Sí," she said. "I *am* Maya. Most people here are. Mi abuelo teaches me. Mi papi helps him when he goes to bless this or that or make rituals, you know? Helps him with his herbs. Abuelito want him to learn, but he . . ."

"Not interested," James tried to fill in the gap.

"No," she confirmed. "No one else. And no one else in the town is interested in our heritage anymore." She frequently grappled with her English. "It is not important to them. But I love it. It is part of me."

He peered out the window into the black, except for the greenery low and aside from the road made visible by headlights. Light gray asphalt and faded lines flowed into them, illuminated in contrast to the darkness. And then, almost as a bright yellow sun in the early night, a diamond-shaped sign reflected ahead and approached rapidly. It was just as any sign of the like that James had seen on a drive along some country road in rural Louisiana, but it was not a deer-crossing sign. The black silhouette was that of a great Central American jaguar. Both men saw it; even stared intently as it passed just as quick, yet neither said a word.

Silence ensued for the remainder of the trek. Only the buzz of the little old four-cylinder engine in need of a tune-up cut the stillness. Brief flashes of moonlight peeked in though the lofty jungle trees and foliage to remind them that not all was quite so dark. It could not penetrate the heart of James Beauregard. There was no comfort there; no brightness of hope. The scowl on his face further soured. His eyebrows dipped sharply as only the negative permeated his thoughts, unstoppable and probably exaggerated.

Soon, there appeared an oasis of dim light in the desert of darkness. A parking lot marked almost a central courtyard between the triangular, thatched visitor's center, a field of covered and preserved ancient statues and carvings, and something to the right that could not yet be identified. Orange overhead lighting reflected an almost Dreamsicle hue from the windshields of scores of vehicles. Marta searched the lot up one row and down another in a near futile search for a spot before she found what might have been the very last parking space on the eve of the vernal equinox.

"Jesus, there are a lot of people here." Tim hung over the seat back before him as the little coupe jolted to a stop. "Tomorrow's a big day."

"Yes," Marta agreed.

"It's still mid-evening," James puzzled as he looked around. "It's going to be a long time before sunrise and the ability to visit the ruins." He paused for half a glimmer of joy that just a short walk through the jungle, and he would be at one of the most important archaeological sites in the world. But the boyish giddiness faded as quickly as it had appeared. "So where the hell are all the people that go with these cars? They can't be in the visitor center. It looks closed."

"There," Marta pointed ahead to the right. "Jaguar Inn."

"Jaguar Inn?" Tim gaped. "There's a hotel out here?"

"Yeah, I didn't see that one coming, either," James said as he observed the facility.

"Is it nice?" Tim turned to Marta. "You seem to have been out here a bunch."

"I do not know," she shrugged. "I have never been inside."

James shot a terrible look at his counterpart, a silent chastisement for the insensitive question. Tim burst with an expression of innocence, surely never to have meant any harm. The moment passed, and silence set for several moments as the men thought.

"He is in there," Marta said as she stared across at the small hotel complex. "Mi Abuelo. They are there, I'm sure. *She* is there," she assured James.

"Are you sure?" He looked with desperate concern into her eyes. "You think so?"

"I can feel it—feel them," she confirmed, softness in her voice.

"Where else would they be, Jimbo?" Tim rationalized. "I wouldn't just sleep in the car if I were them. Hell, I'm ecstatic *we* don't have to. I was *sure* that was the plan."

"Good point." James stewed on it for a moment. "But what does that mean for us? We're here for Noelle. Nothing else. I couldn't give a shit about the jaguar." He saw a look of surprise and growing sadness form on Marta's face.

"So what?" Tim leaned back. "Go in with all guns blazing?"

"You have guns?" Marta seemed worried.

"No," James corrected. "Just an expression."

"Expression?" Her eyebrow rose.

"I mean, do we just go in knocking on doors until we get it right and force our way in?" Tim continued the line of thought. "They actually *do* have guns. And they outnumber us. And they have your fiancée. They could kill us, kill her, kill Marta and her grandfather . . ."

"Reed doesn't seem like the type who wants to kill anyone," James said.

"Okay, fine. Under normal circumstances, I'd agree with you. But he is motivated. He's fulfilling a goal that his society set out on over two hundred years ago. He's *this* close. If you get in his way, there's no telling what he'll do. His son already shot at us, remember?"

James sat in silence for several moments, frequently on the verge of words that did not seem to want to materialize and come forth. He stopped, rubbed his eyes and forehead, and then turned his head to peer out past the windshield at the hotel. He stared for some time, and no one dared break that meditation.

"So what?" James threw up his hand. "Check in? Get a room in the same hotel as Noelle's kidnapper? Like some sort of fucked up, dysfunctional family vacation? That close, and I don't go in and get her?"

"We know where they're going to be in the morning." Tim tried to use a calm voice that might have the same effect on his friend. "We'll get a tourist map to see what trail they might take to the Temple of the Jaguar. So we go out there earlier and wait—"

"In the dark jungle with actual jaguars and snakes that can swallow us whole and then shit us all over the rain forest floor all in one day," he interrupted.

"We wait," Tim ignored the pessimism. "We wait for them and ambush them in the dark."

"They have guns."

"We'll wait till they pass and hit them with a branch or something. Take their guns. It will all be okay."

"I," James paused, distressed, his palms sweaty. "I need a drink." He looked off at the hotel. "Okay, let's get a room." He observed the full lot. "That is if there are any rooms left." He opened the door to exit, as did Tim. "Marta, thank you so very much for your help." James bent over and thanked her graciously. "We could not have come this far without you. Have a safe drive." He stopped as he saw her door swing open.

"I'm staying," she informed them as she stepped out.

"Wait a minute," Tim protested. "You heard what we said. Those men have guns."

"Yes, I know." Her sweet, ethnic demeanor turned fiery and determined. "They were in my home. They waved those guns at me—at my family. Hurt mi papi. They have mi abuelo in that place. They will take him to the temple. His life is in danger like your woman's." She turned to James. "I will stay, and that is final," she insisted, and then marched off toward the hotel.

Chapter 21

A boisterous metallic turn and unlatching was followed by the flick of the light switch to reveal the calm lime hues of the walls within those tight quarters. Earthen tiles nearly clashed with loud, multicolored bedspreads of the three twin beds set up as if a papa, mama, and baby bear would return home at any moment.

"Home sweet home," James filled the room with his voice.

"You didn't even ask—" Tim continued a rant that began soon after check-in.

"I don't want to hear it."

"Didn't even bother to ask," Tim fought for decibel dominance.

"I don't think this place has a Presidential Suite. It's just a little inn."

"But you didn't even ask if they did; find out."

"And who was going to pay for it? I might be made of money, but that doesn't mean I like to always piss it away. Why don't you chip in?" James fired back as Marta stepped across the room with a rolling of her eyes.

"Oh, that's cold. The money. Always rubbing that in."

"Well I feel like I'm always the one that gets the tab."

"Are you two always like this?" Marta asked from the bed at the far side of the room.

"Um," James had to think.

"Yes," Tim jumped in. "Yes, since college. Pledge semester. We roomed together all four years of undergrad, and even into grad school for a while until he moved in with . . ." he stopped short of a sensitive blunder. "Sorry, man."

"Nah." James hung his head and waved off his friend. "It's okay. She existed. I can't run from her memory—hers and Max's. I had the privilege of knowing them and their love, at least for a while. I can't pretend they didn't exist just to save me heartache."

He did not seem to know where to go. He continued to hang his head as solemnity bittered his face. He walked across the room as if to escape to another part of the house, but quickly realized he was not in a house and that there was only a restroom that was separate from the small bed chamber. He stopped and returned, but was met with the presence of his two companions. *Trapped.*

"I need a drink." He shot the gap between the two, yanked open the door, and left the room.

The narrow hallway was more of a tunnel through some dank catacombs. The carpet raised and the walls narrowed as he tried to increase the pace. He was almost at a trot when the hall opened up into a spacious and relief-bringing lobby. Carpet became terra cotta tile he traversed with the clack of his leather soles that carried him past the front desk and to the moderately busy bar area.

He was lucky. The bar seating was sparse, but he found a stool. It was still warm on his rear, so he was very fortunate, indeed. He hated having to sit at tables in a bar unless he was with multiple people. Alone or with one other drinking partner, the bar was the best spot in the house. It was quick access to the booze, and he liked chatting up the barkeep, the most interesting people on the planet. He was never bored with the conversation. Plus, a seat in some dark corner of the bar—he and his thoughts muffled by whiskey—could be dangerous.

"Fuck that," he heard himself utter.

"Pardoname?" the bartender answered.

"Oh, nothing. Whiskey. What do you have?"

"MacAllen," he turned and began to list, but James stopped him.

"That'll do."

"Rocks, señor?"

"Straight," James almost cut him off. *Last thing I need is Montezuma's Revenge.*

As if by magic, the brown room-temperature liquid, a generous three fingers full, was upon the sealed, natural wood bar before him. As a snake that strikes at a mouse, without thought, he snatched up the rocks glass and slugged back the contents in one gulp. The barkeep noticed with his eyebrows raised and a grin that threatened to erupt a chuckle from beneath. He stuffed a slice of lime into the open necks of two freshly cracked cervezas, and then walked over to pour another scotch without even asking if there was a need for it.

"The first one is the quickest," the bartender mused.

"Always." James sipped this one a little more casually. "It's like that first shot of lidocaine."

He felt his nerves calm. The memories drifted as he finished that drink and started another. The warmth glowed from within and he was at ease. He twisted his drink in a circle upon the bar and watched the barkeep distribute libations to patrons from across the globe. But he said not a word, nor did he strike up a conversation with anyone else. He was between dimensions; a ghost that was there, but not there. He observed distantly, but within the crowd. His thoughts were still elsewhere. Heaviness set in.

The droning of the bar crowd suddenly became nearly mute, as if ear plugs were inserted. Things did not look quite right. Faces blurred and movement slowed. New voices filled James's ears with a piercing quality, yet unintelligible. They were whispered and soft, but loud and imposing. Laughter, playful and happy, punctuated the echoed whispers. "There," he heard them say, and then the blurriness was gone; the crowd reinstated.

Nicholas Lockyer Reed strolled across the lobby with confidence and headed toward the front desk, an easy glance away from the bar. James grabbed his drink and pushed away from the bar to fade into the shadows of the lounge. He found a large, square stucco column to back up to, a watchful eye on every move the man made. Nick conducted his business but cast an occasional look over at the bar. James's heart fluttered each time, but nothing indicated that he had been seen.

"Shit." James slid his way around the corner of the column, his head turned sharply to the right and his eyes trained upon Reed.

"What in the hell is he doing?" someone chuckled from a small group of young men at a nearby table. "Playing secret agent?" Laughter erupted.

Smartass college kids. James bit his tongue to respond with something sarcastic. That might draw attention to himself. He watched as the bartender scanned the room. *Damn. I haven't paid yet.* But he dared not move. He watched as his adversary left the front desk and headed full steam toward the bar area. He slunk a little more to the rear, his back flattened even more against the textured stucco as if to meld into it. Reed did not stop at the bar as James had hoped. Instead he walked through the lounge. He panicked as he saw the man headed his way. Sure to keep his back to Reed, James darted out from the column and into the more illuminated recesses of the restroom door.

The damp floors squeaked with the little bit of friction caused by his shoes as he ducked into one of the three stalls. His heart raced, only fueled by the loud yellow ceramic tiles and paint with accents of piercing tropical blue. He sat, but stopped short of the seat to check for any undesirable fluids. With a scowl, he grabbed at the white one-ply toilet paper that dangled from the dispenser, and then dabbed and wiped off a few specks of pale urine before he sat. With only the dingy liquid forming under his feet and the bright yellow stalls to provide scenery, he wondered how long he would have to wait it out. How long should he wait to peek his head from the doorway like a meercat and check to see if it was all clear?

A single set of footsteps echoed within the cramped confines. With nothing but tile and stucco, there was little to absorb sound, so every move, step, throat clearing, and shuffle of clothing was amplified. The stall next to him opened, and through the gap between the door and frame of his own, he could see a sliver of the face that entered. It was Nicholas Reed himself.

The stall door was pulled shut and the latch engaged as James peered under the wall to see which way his shoes would ultimately be pointed. For a moment, they started toward the toilet. And then there was a familiar sound of paper snatched from the dispenser and used to wipe the seat. James knew what was next. The feet on the other side positioned around to the other direction like a waltz, and then with a fluid motion of pants lowering and bent legs, Reed perched himself on the porcelain throne for the long haul.

Before he could act, James heard the rumbles and unpleasant noises from next door. They echoed through the restroom as James placed his hand over his mouth and nose, partially out of disgust, and partially to avoid laughter. He began to stand, but stopped short. *Appearances.* He grabbed for some toilet paper and rubbed it on his pants a bit to mimic the sound of wiping. *No one does it in one wipe.* He repeated it a couple more times for safe measure before he stood, flushed, and bolted out of the restroom and plunged forth toward the bar.

"I thought you left," the bartender said as he approached.

"I wouldn't leave without paying." James quickly drew his wallet, aware of his shortness of time. "El baño, you know?"

"Sí. Another?"

"Uno más," James pulled the cash from the leather folds and paid all that he owed. He smiled as he received his drink and gave a single nod as he pushed off into a far corner of the lounge and a table that was remote and unoccupied. There, he slunk into the chair, his leg crossed upon the other and his eyes on the restroom.

Quite some time passed. James worried about how long it would take for Nicholas to emerge. He might finish his drink prematurely, and then be empty for several minutes. *It would be too risky to go up for another, but there is nothing worse than having an empty whiskey glass.*

After several minutes, Reed did emerge from the restroom and took a sharp right toward the bar where he took up residence on one of the stools. *Crap. He's having a drink.* James took another conservative sip of his dwindling reserves as he watched the bartender grab a pint glass and pour something amber out of one of the taps. *I hope he's a fast drinker. And I hope he's not a lush. We'll be here all damned night. I need another drink.*

He tried to nurse his scotch. He sipped it in small amounts, though it was unnatural for him. He lacked a single conservative bone in his body. Normally, whiskey flowed openly down his throat and without hindrance. He loved its taste. Like a good craft beer, there was a time when he savored it; enjoyed the artisanship of grains and technique. Now he did more gulping than enjoying. A slowed pace of drinking as he waited for his foe to finish should have been a welcome event. Instead, he drummed his fingers on the table as he watched Nicholas and impatiently checked his watch. Impatience turned to frustration. He almost cried out.

To his right, somewhere in the neighborhood of his periphery, movement occurred, and James turned his head to see. Tim Horn meandered almost aimlessly into the lobby. He searched the area in every direction as he stopped, moved, stopped, and moved in different directions. *Shit. He's looking for me. He knows where to find me.* Tim spotted the lounge area and abandoned the wandering search in favor of a more direct approach to the bar.

James sat up, aroused into panic. He looked at Nick, who stared down at his beer for the moment, and then back over at Tim. *He doesn't see him yet. Shit. What to do?* He had to think fast, and the only thing he came up with is to hoist his hands high into the air and wave them with exaggeration. He even half stood from his chair in the shadows to get his friend's attention. *Crap, he doesn't see me. Look this way, moron!* Finally, Tim spotted James.

The waves turned to sweeping directional gestures toward Nicholas at the bar. Tim kept on and their enemy fiddled with his phone, immersed in interactive media and connectedness. Tim slowed his walk, a puzzled look across the face. Shoulders raised, as did hands, in perplexity. *Jesus, don't slow down. Keep walking.* James became more and more exaggerated with is motions, to the point of looking like a football referee until Tim finally shot a glance over at the bar and turned white at the sight of the man who sat there. He turned his head the other way and quickened his pace to almost a trot as he crossed the lounge. Reed looked up from his phone and swigged his beer just as Tim passed and met an emotionally drained James Beauregard.

"Jesus, that was close," Tim half laughed.

"So not funny," James muttered, his face buried in his hands.

"How long have you just been sitting here watching him?"

"A little while." James stared at the foe. "I keep waiting for him to get up and go back to his room so I can follow him, but he hasn't budged."

"Not even to go to the pisser?"

"We've been down that road."

"Wait, you want to follow him back to his room?" Tim said in almost a tone of ridicule. "What happened to ambushing them on the trail in the morning?"

"Why? We have a chance now. We know they're here. If we know which room they're in, maybe we can find a way to get Noelle out tonight and make a run for it in Marta's car." He paused a moment as Tim thought it over.

"No live jaguars in the hotel. I don't want to go out into the rain forest when it's dark either. So what's the plan?"

"Dunno. I haven't gotten past the follow-him-to-his-room phase. Like I said, he hasn't moved. He just sits there. Alone." James began an exaggerated London Cockney dialect. "Oh, pour me anotha, gov'nah," he mocked.

"Pretty sure he doesn't talk like that."

"Me glass is already empty," James continued with a smirk. "I'm so bloody smart and cultured with me accent and me exotic red ale."

"You're being ethnocentric," Tim said with an emotionless face.

"And the way I say *compu-uh*. And *wa-uh*. I spilled wa-uh on me compu-uh, gov'nah."

"This is why British people hate Americans. So if you're quite done, he's paying his tab."

"Oh shit." James snapped into seriousness. "Okay, let's be careful and keep our distance."

They crept across the dark, carpeted bar area as they watched the man stride the distance of the lobby. They watched as he rounded the corner to disappear into the hallway, and then sped their pace to catch up. They trotted across the tile to the corner of the corridor as the desk clerk gazed at them with perplexity. They stood at the edges and peeked their heads around to catch a glimpse before retracting.

Reed continued to walk, ever distanced from the professors. They sprinted down a portion of the hallway and ducked left beside the ice maker. They peeked again before they moved further down the hall to take refuge in the elevator area. As they peered around the corner, they watched Reed disappear into the second-to-last room on the right.

"There it is." James led his friend down the hall to the room. "One eighty-eight."

"All right, let's get the hell out of here before someone comes back out to go to the vending machine or something," Tim said as they scurried back down the corridor. "What's the plan?"

"Let's go back to the room. We'll figure it out there."

Chapter 22

Small plastic wheels chirped as they rolled and toggled under a small cart that headed down the red-carpeted corridor. With a white linen drape, the cart was an apparition that lacked the grace of a spirit as it screamed like a banshee past door after closed door. It came to a rest near the end of the hallway at room one hundred eighty-eight and its operator, a petite young Guatemalan woman in plain blue housekeeping garb stepped out from behind it only to stop short of the door. Marta stared at the number and then the door. She did not move for many seconds as she breathed in deeply and exhaled to calm her nerves. She stepped and rapped lightly.

"Who is it?" a gruff, British voice answered after some startled rustling. The door rattled as someone's face pressed against it to peer through the peep hole. "It looks like room service," the voice whispered, and after a few more moments the door opened.

"Comida," Marta squeaked, her hands clasped behind her back. Her eyes widened and bulged with anxiety as the young Englishman inspected her. She prayed that he would not recognize her.

"Yes, it looks like room service." He looked over at the covered plate. "Who?" He turned to find an answer with the company he kept. He looked over his father, Noelle in a chair across the room, an attentive Rupert, and the old shaman. "Who ordered," he inquired, having not even looked at it. He lifted the lid and studied the food with an upturned nose. "I don't even know what the hell his is. What is this?" he questioned the young woman.

"No Ingles," she shook her head.

"This." He gestured impatiently to the food. "What the hell is this food?"

"Oh, sí. Chuchitos."

"What is a Chuchito?" he snapped.

"It's like a little tamale," Noelle spoke from across the room.

"Oooh, tamales," Rupert beamed.

"No one ordered this." Dr. Reed approached the doorway, but to a blank face on the young woman. "We didn't order this. We're not paying—" He stopped short with the realization that she did not understand a word. "I'm going to the desk." He stormed past her with a scowl and disappeared down the hall.

Rupert had, by then, stood from his position on the bed and begun to examine the food with boyish giddiness. "And plantains," he said with excitement. He took hold of the cart and started to pull it into the room. Marta had now achieved invisibility.

Across the hall, just out of view from the doorway, a steel doorknob turned. It made a few light screeches, followed by the sound of a latch free of the door jam. The heavy metal stairwell door creaked open just far enough for James and Tim to slip through and creep forth to hide along the wall, out of sight. Marta tried not to move her head. She retained her meek, servantly demeanor, hands still behind her back, and head lowered.

The cart remained partially in the entrance to the room to prop open the door. James looked back at Tim and then down the hallway to make sure Reed was not on his way back. With a deep breath, James mustered all his rage and grabbed the handles of the cart. His legs pushed forth as an offensive lineman as the cart crashed ahead with food and plates sent airborne and in every direction. Rupert, his mouth still full and lips coated in greasy deliciousness, reeled and crashed hard to the floor under the wrath of the food cart.

James let go of the cart as Nick leapt to his feet. His head snapped left and eyes caught sight of the pistol on the TV stand. He dashed for it as James chugged forth and lowered his center of gravity. He dug his shoulder bones as deep as he could into Nick Reed's chest, and sent the man to his back before he could grab for the gun.

"Marta," the old man said, worried for his granddaughter as he watched her step back as far across the hall and away from danger as she could get.

Rupert struggled to throw aside the metal cart, linen, and bits of food. He rolled and gyrated on the floor as a turtle on his back until he could finally position himself and fight to get to his feet. He reached for the gun only to be tackled from the side by Tim. They fell solidly to the carpeted floor as each set of adversaries angled and fought for the upper hand. Tim landed hefty punches to Rupert's kidneys, causing the man to grimace and grab Tim's wrists. They rolled and maneuvered, wallowing in greasy Chuchitos as James and Nick drew blood.

Nick's right fist, tight and menacing, cracked across James's face. James struggled beneath the weight of his foe. Punch after punch landed before James could catch his wrists and stop the barrage. Nick utilized his weight and pushed James's hands to the floor to pin him.

"I'm going to fucking kill you," Nick screamed as blood dripped from his lip, mixed with saliva. His eyes were filled with hate and his face a Satanic red.

James looked deep into those enraged eyes and calmly moved his left leg over Nick's. With the leg immobilized, he quickly stretched his left arm, Nick's fists still firmly affixed, as far north of his head as he could. With a quick shift of weight and Nick's left leg and arm useless, James rolled over to pin him. Every ounce of anger came to the surface and that manifested in his fists. Blow after blow struck a nearly defenseless face until halted by a familiar metallic sound. The slide of a semi-automatic pistol chimed and chambered a round. James turned his head to see that Noelle had possession of the gun. He smiled as he and Tim stood up from their defeated foes.

"Let's get the fuck out of here," James struggled with his breath, his eyes on a writhing and nearly unconscious Nick Reed.

But as he turned, he saw that Noelle was not pointing the gun at Nick or Rupert. Instead, it was lowered, and then it was being handed over to Rylan Reed, whose own gun's barrel made a ringed impression into the skin of Noelle's left temple.

"If you two are quite done." He took the gun from Noelle's hand and pushed her to the ground in front of her as Nick and Rupert labored to their feet. "We have an early appointment with the gods."

Chapter 23

The blanket of pre-dawn dark, heavy as a quilt, could suffocate a person in the humidity. Each step down the narrow dirt path was unsure with an occasional rock or uneven spot. The beams from the military-style flashlights did little to illuminate their surroundings as they shot through sight-saving red lenses. Their steps crunched the grit beneath them at a rhythmic pace that kept the beat behind the orchestra of sounds made by the deep Central American rainforest. The array of insect chirps set the key with occasional filler melodies provided by monkeys and birds hidden by the black. A sudden rustle in the brush startled the prisoners who marched in front of their British captors.

"Jesus, what was that?" James jumped.

"Probably a jaguar," Tim mused.

"Shut the f—" James was interrupted.

"Tim, stop it," Noelle sanctioned.

"Thank you," James said.

"I wouldn't be worried about jaguars. They keep to themselves," she continued. "It's the giant tarantulas. Probably everywhere in the early morning like this. Big hairy ones with a red abdomen."

"You guys suck."

"Quiet," Dr. Reed commanded in a low, authoritarian tone.

"I'm sorry," James whispered to Noelle.

"Sorry?"

"For fucking this up."

"What did you fuck up?" she asked.

"Trying to get you out of that room."

"I love you so much." She grasped his hand. "How many men out there would have flown thousands of miles and fought armed kidnappers to try and rescue me? You tried. That's all that matters."

As he felt her warm, soft hand in his, he was stricken with guilt. His chest felt as if it would cave in under the emotion. He thought of his late wife and son. Betrayal. But then for his thoughts of Noelle. *I don't know if I can marry her. I don't want to make a mistake. Break her heart because I can't let go. But if I don't marry her . . . she'll be devastated.* The sound of a pistol slide and the chambering of a round shook his thoughts.

"I said quiet," Dr. Reed ordered.

"And don't even think about trying to scamper off." Rupert found his rare opportunity to wield power.

Silently, the group continued their march into dark, open, nothingness, despair the anticipated conclusion. Dark became dim. The leaves of the canopy above, once non-visible, formed black, connected silhouettes against the barely-lit gray that shone between. They swayed in the early breeze to ever change form; melancholy expressions upon nature's canvas.

New sounds began faint. The rapid beats of indigenous drums and chants in ancient tongues rode in on the smells of smoke that pillowed from sacred flames. They coursed on the air like an apparition of the souls who had occupied this land a thousand years before. Those spirits surrounded and became stronger as the group drew near the central acropolis. The sounds of the drums, traditional woodwinds, and chants echoed from one stone wall to another as James and the rest passed the decayed remnants of once majestic palaces and cast their gaze high to the still shadowy monument before them.

"The Temple of the Jaguar." The words slid from James's mouth.

They followed the path around the northern side and into the main plaza where a great fire raged in the center between the identical facing temples—the Temple of the Masks to the west and the Temple of the Jaguar to the east. The stone, tiered pyramids reached sharply toward the brightening heavens, the doorways to the ritual chambers now visible at the top of each. The gray and white weathering were as scars that told the tales of a millennia of stories still present in the energy that seemed to flow through the place. With feathered wings and headdresses, men danced with ancient grace about the fire, as they willed their spirits touch the hands of the gods on high via the smoke that rose from the center of the plaza. Long loincloths dragged and flowed below unclothed abdomens as they moved about almost in a trance-like state. And then they stopped, all eyes upon the visitors.

"Oh shit." Nick eyed them nervously as the group approached the plaza and the steps to the Temple of the Jaguar. "Are they going to attack?" his voice quivered as he gripped his gun.

"Jesus, they're not savages," James said. "They're probably school teachers and cab drivers on any other day."

"But they might contact the authorities." Dr. Reed also eyed them with suspicion.

"They will not," Abuelito said. "They will not interfere. They know *He* has returned, and so they will let him return."

James rolled his eyes. Faces among the group ranged from reverence to skepticism. And then there was optimism. The old Ah Kin was calm, and even chipper in the face of what the others considered a dire occasion. With another long stare at the silenced ritual group in the plaza, the captors nudged their prisoners along to the left and followed them as they approached the bottom of the pyramid steps.

"It's a funerary temple, yes?" Dr. Reed admired.

"Sí," Abuelito said. "Nine levels." He pointed to the tiers. "Nine levels of the underworld. Jasaw Chan K'awiil, who is buried within, hoped this temple would connect him directly with the gods and the next world. Bring him into the next life."

James, along with his captured crew, stopped short of the first of many steps. The deep green grass almost gripped the stone all the way down, as if to hold it in place. It was gray-white, weathered with eons of summer and spring rainstorms and sweltering humidity. He turned his eyes upward. The stairs climbed into the territory of the gods. It towered and lorded over the rest of the buildings, the trees, and the wildlife that surely filled the forest. It was a giant; a god itself living, yet dormant among the mortal world.

And then the first step. The sky ever brightened as their legs lifted and churned up each decayed stone level. Muscles burned and ached with only the dull and gray before them to see. James dared not deviate. After every passing minute, they ascended this mountain with no rails, ropes, or harnesses to stop a potential tumble down the pyramid. He could feel his knees weaken and his fatigued thighs quiver as he tried to focus on each step, rather than the lofty position above the jungle canopy. He was conscious of his breathing. It was deliberate and exaggerated. He tried to occupy his mind with less important things. Before long, they had reached the top and the darkened entrance to the temple upon high.

"Hard to imagine." Dr. Reed turned, his hands snug in his pockets. He gazed out over the newly visible canopy and the other buildings in the complex. "This place must have been magnificent a thousand years ago, not that it isn't now. It's hard to imagine its pre-ruin condition. The temples. The homes. People carrying out their daily lives. Why, on this very spot, blood was often spilled. In the name of some greater cause, average people were sacrificed—a blood offering and then the bodies would be tossed down these steps in disregard." He turned and gave a sinister smile as he met eyes with his captives. Then he moved past them toward the temple entrance.

He stopped and, without a word, reached for Nick's backpack. Nick positioned himself so that his father could more easily access the back. The lanyard was pulled and the pocket opened. And from within, Reed retrieved the cloth-wrapped jaguar. He removed its swaddling to expose the stone to the virgin sunlight. James watched with stern, unemotional eyes as the professor moved slowly to the doorway. All he could think of was a way to make a run for it. *Futility*. But the old shaman next to him beamed with joy, a perpetual smile upon his face.

"For the first time in centuries, He is home," the old man said as the group of captives followed the British men into the small confines of the stone temple.

For everything the temple could boast in ingenuity, it lacked in flash. The small, plain room formed a sharp, triangular ceiling that ran high into the roof comb atop the shrine that, on the exterior, once bore the seated likeness of the king. The chipped off-white plaster covered most of the walls with the limestone visible in some areas. A faint light-green paint gave hint that the shrine was once quite decorative.

"Place is kind of a dump," Tim's voice echoed.

"It's been recycled by later invading Mayan groups," James said. "Plundered by them and whoever came after. There were paintings of the king and the gods. All faded. The carved wood lintels are long gone. Two of them are in the British Museum." He caught a hateful glance from Nick Reed. "Bastards don't even have it on display. They're in a box somewhere in the fucking basement."

"The jaguar," Dr. Reed uttered, no attention paid to the banter. "Where does it go? What do I do with it? Anything special? There's no socket or anything where it rests? No pedestal?" His voice turned impatient as he spun around with rage in his eyes. He shouted at the old shaman. "Where? Answer me!"

"The chosen seeks to control his fate," the old man recited. "He seeks his blessing from the realm of the gods on high where Bahlam resides. When the sun wakes on the day of equal light and dark, the chosen communes with him and will receive his blessing. There." His finger lifted and he pointed to a small, square opening in the wall.

Reed approached it. He stretched his neck, and with a keen eye, peered through to the outside of the temple. He could see light born of the first rays of dawn already beginning to illuminate the insides of the stone hole with rich, golden morning beams.

"He returns to the light," the shaman said. "But you must not," he said, though Reed was not listening. "You are not chosen."

As the sun crowned the horizon high above the tree line and aligned with the portal in the temple shrine, the air changed. Everything changed inside the shrine while the rest of the world remained unaffected. Every molecule in every stone, human body, and even the air vibrated at such a speed as to each make a microscopic incision in the fabric of space and time. It was as a giant, low-frequency soundwave without any amplitude to damage the ears. Teeth gnashed and eyes clenched in response to pain that did not actually occur on a neurological level.

"Come, Nicholas!" Reed beamed as he moved for the portal with the stone jaguar in his hand. "This is part of your family heritage, too."

"But," James protested, stunned and a bit frightened, "what if . . . ?"

"Bahlam has made his choice," the shaman said, and calmly lifted his hand.

The Reed men lifted the jaguar together, each with a hand upon it, and hoisted it to the portal to bathe it in the rays of the equinox sun. Spellbound, James watched as their eyes of reverence and wonder became eyes of fear, and then terror. Dr. Reed's mouth gaped and his breathing became labored. He and his son seemed to want to release the stone jaguar but could not. Nick's eyes rolled back to leave the whites exposed only while his father convulsed and shook, and then the both of them collapsed to the floor.

The others took a jolted step back. Rupert fell to his bottom with a frantic scoot in reverse and against the far wall as he eyed his two companions lifeless on the floor. The jaguar lay between them as the environment within the room continued to vibrate with increased violence.

"Hurry," the old shaman said to James. "You must return Him. There is little time. He has chosen you."

James stood frozen in shock for several moments. He feared to move, his gaze upon the two dead men and the idol that seemed to cause it. He locked eyes with the shaman. He felt the warmth and reassurance exuded by the medicine man. Calm surrounded and insulated him from harm. He was at ease and then moved for the jaguar as if pulled to it by some other force. He grasped it with both hands and approached the portal. As he hoisted it into the sunlight, he felt himself in a completely different place.

He looked around to see his home. It was still and quiet. Everything was perfect; nothing out of place. The blood-red wood floors shined with a recent polish. Potpourri coursed on the air. Light cascaded in through the windows, channeled in by the curtains that framed them. And then footsteps. They were rapid. They resonated within the hollow space under the floorboards as if a stampede had begun in his home. From down the hall came a little boy in blue pajamas. He scampered with glee, his face bright with joy as he caught sight of his father. With a burst of energy, he sprinted for James and crashed into his legs before gripping them like a python.

"Daddy!" he shouted.

James dropped to his knees and engulfed the boy in his arms. His mouth hung open without a single word, though so many tried to leak out. He trembled, tears in rivers down his face. He closed his eyes and wept over his son as he listened to another set of footsteps from across the house.

"Mommy," Max called out. "Daddy's here."

"Honey, what's wrong?" Abigail appeared from the next room.

James stood as his heart threatened to leap from his chest. He quivered to see his late wife glide with barefooted grace in her bright cream nightgown. It glowed, crowned by her gilded, dirty-blond hair and honey-touched complexion. She placed her hand gently on his forearm, but he abruptly embraced and pulled her within his bosom. As he sobbed on her shoulder, her pleasant expression barely changed. She pulled away from him enough to look him in the eyes and take his face in her hands.

"James," she spoke as an angel, "what's the matter? Why are you crying?"

"I love you," he managed to say. "I love you both so much."

His eyes took in the beautiful sight. Happiness mingled with anguish, and longing for this moment to last forever. *This is what the heart wants. Somehow, He knows that.* But then the stares of his wife and child were somehow emotionless. They did not reflect the tragedy that had, in reality, befallen them. This was an alternate reality where the accident did not happen. And then his experiences afterward would never happen the way they did. *Change my history. Change theirs. Control my fate.* He thought for a moment, and again took in the almost blank stares of his family. *But what about the fate of others? How would this change the rest of the world? The lives of others? For good? For the worse?*

And then he thought of Noelle. She became all he could think of, even with his late wife and child still in his embrace. So much joy and beauty had entered his life with her there. He had a future; not a past to think of. Progression. No longer did it feel like cheating on Abigail and Max. Acceptance. It was life. Perhaps it was fate; a higher purpose. Perhaps there was more in this world to do.

"Goodbye." He stepped away from his family and his former life. "I release you. And you release me. I will love you always." Tears rolled down his face as he waved goodbye with the acknowledgment that he would never again see them in the flesh.

He was now surrounded by the ancient stone walls of the temple shrine. The vibrations had stopped. Everything turned still and the sun had risen above the horizon, and no longer filled the portal in the stone wall. There within the opening stood the jaguar, at home and at peace.

"He smiles on you," the shaman said in an almost bowing gesture. "Thank you. Thank you."

"How long was I gone?" James said, a bit disoriented.

"Gone? You never left," Tim half chuckled.

"You just put the jaguar up there, and all the—whatever all that was—stopped," Noelle said.

James rushed to her and took her in his arms, which caught her off-guard at first. But she felt his love. It flowed from his body to hers and she melted into him with mutual affection.

"Is everything okay?" she asked, worried for him.

"Perfect," he said as he found that special place in her eyes. "Everything is perfect. Let's go home."

"You've got a lot to explain to the authorities about two dead men up here at a World Heritage Site, Rupert," Tim said with a gesture to the Reed men lifeless on the floor.

"Think of all the people who are going to be here on the day of the equinox." James took Noelle under his arm and walked out with the rest. "Good luck with that."

And the five of them left Rupert in the shrine with a panicked expression as they descended the steps. The grateful eyes of the ritual group below thanked them silently as they came down from the heavens, a peace over this place rarely ever experienced by anyone anywhere.

Epilogue

The front door squeaked open and closed again with reverberation throughout the old French Quarter house. The floorboards creaked under James's weight as he crossed the house and entered the kitchen. With a careless toss, his keys clanged against the granite countertop and slid to a halt.

"Hey baby," Noelle popped as she walked in from the living room. "Get Tim off on his way back to New Haven?"

"Indeed," James said, and pulled at her waist and gave her a kiss. "He says he's ready for a *real* adventure—enduring these undergrads for the long, no-holiday stretch from here until the end of the semester."

"He isn't kidding." She rolled her eyes. "I'm not ready for spring break to be over."

"But with spring breaks like this . . ."

"Yeah, normal and mundane is sort of welcome at this point."

James could hear the news playing in the living room. "Authorities in Guatemala say that two strange deaths occurred this week in Tikal . . ."

"What is that, local or national?" James started in that direction.

"Um, national," Noelle guessed and followed with interest.

"The two bodies were discovered in the shrine at the top of the Temple of the Great Jaguar, here at this extremely important ancient Mayan site," the female anchor reported as images from the scene crossed the screen. "They have been identified as Nicholas Reed and his father, Dr. Rylan Reed, a professor and minor academic celebrity who has contributed to a number of educational programs. They seem to have had no struggle, nor is foul play suspected, but the mysterious circumstances surrounding the death of both men, the location, and the holy Mayan day on which the death occurred raise suspicions. At least one living associate discovered at the scene is under further interrogation."

James and Noelle grinned at each other almost in disbelief as the report ended with the same lack of intense interest as it began. It would likely never again be mentioned on the news. It would fade into oblivion as a story. James turned his attention back to the screen for a brief moment and caught a glimpse of the anchor who had read the story. His heart nearly fell from his chest into his abdomen as the studied the face of the woman. His mouth hung open as his eyes moved quickly to a framed photo of his late wife and child upon the desk, and then back to the screen.

"I'm Abby Wheeler, and this is CBC News," she smiled.

Acknowledgments

My wife Melissa Richardson, who has always supported this boyish dream. My mother, Debbie Richardson, who has always encouraged me to be creative and work hard. My editor Jim Koukis. He's always so easy to work with and truly enjoys helping to polish a great story. Jessica Kristie, who believed in my work and was determined to whip me into shape as an author. Sherry Foley, for her tough love and always seeking to make me a better writer. Thanks to the numerous family members who have believed in me. Al Barron and the Washington Parish Library for the enormous support and opportunities. My friend Glyn Hays who has read every manuscript before even my publisher. One of my oldest friends and one of my earliest fans, Dr. Steve Landreneau. Trayce Moore for her friendship and early support of my career. Thanks for hooking me up with the newspaper attention. Chuck Carter, ever the valued sounding board for ideas. And the city of New Orleans for the never ending inspiration.

About the Author

J.M. Richardson is a native of southeast Louisiana. He is continuously inspired by the culture and people of the Greater New Orleans area, and frequently sets his stories there. He is an alumnus of Louisiana State University for his bachelor's degree and the University of North Texas for his Master's. He now resides in the Fort Worth, TX, area with his wife and two daughters where he teaches psychology, sociology, and macroeconomics.

www.ingramcontent.com/pod-product-compliance
Lightning Source LLC
Chambersburg PA
CBHW020907180626
46816CB00007BA/2277